D0861250

COI
THE HOO   ER FILES

COLUMBO:
THE HOOVER FILES

William Harrington

Chivers Press • G.K. Hall & Co.
Bath, England   Thorndike, Maine USA

This Large Print edition is published by Chivers Press, England, and by G.K. Hall & Co., USA.

Published in 2000 in the U.K. by arrangement with Universal.

Published in 2000 in the U.S. by arrangement with Chivers Press, Ltd.

U.K. Hardcover ISBN 0-7540-4010-0 (Chivers Large Print)
U.K. Softcover ISBN 0-7540-4011-9 (Camden Large Print)
U.S. Softcover ISBN 0-7838-8925-9 (Nightingale Series Edition)

COLUMBO: THE HOOVER FILES
A novel by William Harrington
Based on the Universal Television Series COLUMBO
Created by Richard Levinson & William Link

The text of this Large Print edition is unabridged.
Other aspects of the book may vary from the original edition.

Set in 16 pt. New Times Roman.

Printed in Great Britain on acid-free paper.

British Library Cataloguing in Publication Data available

Library of Congress Cataloging-in-Publication Data

Harrington, William, 1931–
    Columbo : the Hoover files / William Harrington.
       p.   cm.
    ISBN 0-7838-8925-9 (lg. print : sc : alk. paper)
    1. Columbo, Lieutenant (Fictitious character)—Fiction.
    2. Hoover, J. Edgar (John Edgar), 1895–1972—Fiction.
    3. Police—California—Los Angeles—Fiction.   4. Los Angeles (Calif.)—Fiction.   5. Large type books.   I. Title.
PS3558.A63 C66   2000
813'.54—dc21   99–056672

PART ONE

'That guy there. That guy in the raincoat. That's Lieutenant Columbo, LAPD Homicide. He never misses. He'll get whoever did it. If I was the guy that blew up Betsy, I'd be shakin' in my shoes.'

1

WEDNESDAY, DECEMBER 16—2:41 P.M.

Though this was the fourth time she had visited the place, Betsy Clendenin could never enter this California women's prison without a shudder. The women's stares—many curious, some wistful, some hostile—distressed her. She knew what she was to them: a handsome, well-dressed, confident woman, free to come and go. They were conspicuously envious, most of them, of her fur-collared beige suede coat and would be more envious if they could see her royal blue suede mini-dress. She was conscious—no, *self*-conscious—of the contrast between her and them.

'I read your latest, Miss Clendenin,' said the uniformed woman officer who conducted her across the campus, into the building that housed the visiting facility. 'Tough stuff. I had no idea. I supposed Jonathan was a real straight talented guy.'

'They say celebrity is its own reward, that you can get away with anything if you're a celebrity and pile up enough money. And it is that way until somebody finds you out and exposes you.'

'I read somewhere that his latest disk isn't selling at all. I guess people are turned off on

3

him.'

'Disgusted is the word.'

I expect Mrs. Cooper-Svan will be glad to see you.'

'I'm always glad to see her. I'm damned sorry she's here.'

'Hey, *I'm* sorry she's here. I guess we're all sorry she's here. But you beat your husband's brains out, you wind up in this kind of place. Particularly if Lieutenant Columbo works your case. We got two other women here because of Lieutenant Colombo. Remember Erika Björling, the gameshow squealer? She's here for the same reason: Lieutenant Columbo. He's got a rep in this place.'

'Gunnar Svan had it coming,' said Betsy Clendenin.

'I figure he did,' said the officer. 'Which is why she got ten years instead of life.'

'She still working in the cafeteria?'

'Yeah. Doesn't seem to want any other kind of job. Actually, her real work is what she does in her cell. Reads. Marks up manuscripts—editing, I guess you call it. You know, she's got a typewriter, writes some stuff; I don't know what. Technically, she's not supposed to run a business from here, so I guess we've bent the rules a little for her. She's taken it hard, being here. I hate to think what her time here would do to her if we didn't let her run her magazine from her cell.'

'She doesn't actually run it,' said Betsy. 'She

4

couldn't. What she does is some editing, and she makes some choices and decisions about what will be published. Also, she writes a column that's published under another name. But the day-to-day operations—of course, she still *owns* it.'

'She's a rich woman. She's going to have a good life when she's paroled in two, three more years. All of us here wish her well.'

*   *   *

Ai-ling Cooper-Svan did not thrive on imprisonment. Except when she was working in her cell, she was lethargic—just enduring, doing her time. Having been here as long as she had and having no bad marks on her record, she was entitled to wear street clothes; but she didn't; she wore the blue denim jumpsuit the institution issued her. The straight black hair she had always kept so carefully styled now simply hung around her ears, just cut, with no style at all. She was of course descended from generations of Chinese women, and from generations of Yankee sea captains who had married those Chinese women—so her face was round; she had a pug nose and black eyes. She had gained a little weight, which showed even through the jumpsuit. She shook hands with Betsy and sat down at a square wooden table. Immediately she pulled a package of Marlboros from her

5

pocket and used a paper match to light a cigarette.

'Bill told me you've got something for me,' said Ai-ling Cooper, who was trying to drop the Svan, the name of the abusive husband she had killed. 'Got it with you?'

Betsy gestured to the officer who was examining the contents of her little briefcase. The woman brought the briefcase to the table and handed it to her. Betsy pulled out a manuscript.

'Who's getting it in the balls this time?' asked Ai-ling.

'John Edgar Hoover,' said Betsy with a little smile.

'Been done, hasn't it?'

'Not what *I've* got. When I publish what I've got, they'll take his name off the FBI building in Washington.'

'What's this, a chapter?'

'A chapter. I can't let you have the hottest stuff just yet. I've got to save something to make the book sell. But what I've got here will work for *Glitz.*'

'We've always done well by each other,' said Ai-ling. 'How many pieces have you run in *Glitz*? Six?'

'Six.'

'Right—including two you've brought here to my luxury retreat.'

'What you need is a pardon.'

'Well—Maybe it's not impossible. I've made

6

Glitz more political since I've been here. You know, figuring maybe I could build up some influence. Off the record.'

'Of course.'

'You see the cartoon?'

Ai-ling referred to a cartoon that appeared in a San Francisco paper after *Glitz* magazine made its first political endorsement. The cartoon showed the endorsed candidate kneeling outside Ai-ling's cell while she reached through the bars with a sword and dubbed him knight.

Ai-ling picked up the manuscript Betsy had brought her and glanced at it. She grinned as she read—

Eleanor Roosevelt called them 'disgusting.' FDR had to be at some pains to prevent her saying publicly that she found the openly erotic relationship between J. Edgar Hoover and his boyfriend Clyde Tolson nauseating.

Why was Hoover not forced out of the closet? Because by the time he and Tolson arrogantly flaunted their homosexuality, the Director had become so powerful that he supposed he could do anything he wished, without fear of disclosure or criticism.

Almost everyone who knew the facts and could have exposed him was under threat of blackmail. Director Hoover had for years used the FBI as a personal fiefdom, and much of the work of its agents was given over to building dossiers against anyone he regarded as a potential enemy. Much of the 'information' contained in those files was gossip at best, outright fraud in many instances, but it was 'information' its subjects did not want publicized by the powerful—and eminently (though fraudulently) credible—Director of the Federal Bureau of Investigation.

Fraud? Yes. John Edgar Hoover was never the anti-Communist zealot he trumpeted himself to be. His FBI was ineffective against subversion. He pretended to be anti-Communist to distract attention from the fact that he had entered into an unholy alliance with the Mob, agreeing to lay off organized crime in return for . . . God knows what.

Ai-ling put down the manuscript: some thirty pages. 'You've got a deal,' she said. I may change a word or two, but you've got a deal.'

'I've got a whole lot more than what you see there,' said Betsy. 'A whole lot worse. I've got information to the effect that Hoover disclosed confidential FBI files to Roy Cohn, to help him in his defense against criminal charges. I'm trying to get in touch with a retired agent named Kloss, who may know something about it. He was assigned to FBI headquarters in Washington when this came down. He doesn't want to talk to me, but he's gonna have to.'

'Bring me some of *that*, and we've got a real big-money deal. Meanwhile, don't talk so much on TV,' said Ai-ling. 'I want at least *some* of this stuff to be new when we run it.'

2

8:02 P.M.

Betsy pointed her garage-door opener and pressed the button. The lights went on in the garage, and then the door rose. She picked up from the seat another radio controller and pressed the button on that one. It switched on bright floodlights that glared on the front of the house. Her shrubbery was all small. No one could be crouching behind a shrub. She kept nothing in the garage behind which anyone could hide. Satisfied that all was clear, she drove in and used the controller to close the door behind her.

Betsy took no chances. Over the years she had offended a lot of people. Offended? No, much more than that; she had exposed them to ridicule, censure, and even to prosecution. She could have no doubt there were people in this world who would like to kill her. Or at the very least to give her a savage beating.

Three had tried. None had ever touched her. She carried a pistol, knew how to use it, and had no hesitation about using it. She had

9

in fact shot one man in the leg.

She used her key to open the door between the garage and kitchen. She then had twenty seconds to step to the control panel and enter a code. If she did not, the whole house would erupt in the ear-splitting screams of four horns, and the alarm company would put in a call to the police. She punched in the code, then went to the counter and poured herself a glass of Scotch, to which she added ice and no soda. She walked into the living room and switched on the lights on the Christmas tree before she went upstairs to change.

Betsy Clendenin was forty-two years old and was a full-figured, husky, vigorous woman who tended to move faster than she needed to, sometimes trotting up the stairs. Tonight she walked up. She had driven to the prison and back and was feeling a little weary. She shed her clothes and stood looking at herself in the bathroom mirror, a little resentful of the red marks elastic had left on her skin. She took a moment to brush her hair. It was light brown but frosted with bleach carefully applied by her hairdresser. She wiped off her makeup. It had been on too long. She liked to go naked inside her house. She picked up a dressing gown and carried it downstairs, in case someone came to the door.

She had drunk her Scotch while upstairs, so went to the kitchen and poured another. She lit a cigarillo.

Time to check her telephone recorder. She had five messages, all but one routine. That was—

'Miss Clendenin, this is Frederick Kloss . . . uh, returning your call. You can call me again tomorrow if you want.'

Curt and hostile. Apart from the curtness of the message, hostility put a sharp edge on his voice. Kloss didn't want to talk to her. But he would because, like a lot of other people, he did not want her to write of him that he would not return her telephone calls or that he refused to be interviewed. He was smart enough to know that was tantamount to a damaging admission.

Betsy returned to her kitchen. She explored the refrigerator, looking for something to eat. She would love to go out to a restaurant, even alone, but she was tired. No question. She was tired. She had frozen pizzas. Those were her fall-back dinners. She would have a small pizza, with a tomato-and-onion salad, and red wine. Okay. Not a bad end to a long day.

But too early. She carried her Scotch in the living room, sat down naked on her couch and for several minutes just stared at her Christmas tree. Then she picked up the clicker and began to surf the television channels.

If there was satisfaction in seeing yourself on the tube, she'd had all that satisfaction she could want. Actually, it was too late now for the shows where her name might be mentioned. The networks were on their usual bullskevitch. She looked for a good movie. And found one. The original *Dracula*, starring Bela Lugosi. She'd seen it twenty times, but she chose it. 'Your will is *strong* . . . Van . . . Helsing.' Betsy relaxed and sipped Scotch.

Her mind was not monopolized. She thought about Kloss. Of course, he didn't want to talk to her. He might have information on the Director that would destroy the pitiful remaining shreds of that old, grotesquely inflated reputation. The Roy Cohn connection. And more.

Kloss was squirming. Okay. She'd make him squirm more.

3

THURSDAY, DECEMBER 17—6:42 A.M.

Frederick Kloss—Fritz—sat down over his breakfast of orange juice with one ice cube in the glass, bacon and eggs, toast, and coffee, the same breakfast he had eaten every morning for the past sixty years. He ate alone. His wife of thirty-four years had been dead almost twenty years. He spread his newspaper on the table and glanced through it as he ate. He always looked for any story recounting some new exploit by the Federal Bureau of Investigation.

He had been an agent of the FBI for

12

twenty-five years, from 1949 to 1974. It was the defining experience of his life. He was seventy-five years old now and had been retired from the agency more years than he had served it, but he still identified himself as an FBI man. In spite of the fact that after retirement from the FBI he'd made a fortune in Los Angeles County real estate, he did not think of himself as a realtor. Like an old fraternity brother, he attended every agents' reunion or convention he could, and he made a point of stopping by the Los Angeles office every month or so, to be sure they knew who he was and to compare the way things now were with the way they had been.

Everything was very different now, mostly in ways he could not approve. He had seen agents wearing sweatshirts and jeans, with baseball caps! There were women agents! There was a want of the discipline and respect, plus the unfailing self-confidence, that had so characterized the FBI in the old days and had been a key to its effectiveness.

Fritz Kloss still wore three-piece suits in winter, two-piece suits in summer, always with white shirts and narrow ties. He wore felt hats in winter, straw hats in summer. That was what the Director had prescribed. (Once when he mentioned the old dress code to one of the young men in the office, the fellow had made an unfunny joke: 'Yeah, you guys had to dress like the Fruit of Islam.')

13

He had retired two years after the Director died. The FBI had already begun to deteriorate. And it had deteriorated sadly every year since.

That had been inevitable. No organization could lose a leader like the Director and fail to weaken. Director Hoover had *been* the FBI. He had shaped and guided it and made it the world's preeminent law-enforcement agency. No agency anywhere had even approached it. The FBI under the Director had been America's pride, the world's envy.

He'd had the privilege of knowing the Director personally. For eight years he had worked at SOG, the FBI term meaning 'Seat of Government.' Knowing the Director would be looking at him, he'd kept his hair trimmed, his suits cleaned and pressed, his shoes shined; he'd even had his hat blocked. He never wore a white shirt twice between launderings. Each time he spoke with the Director, he made a point of focusing his entire attention on him, catching not just the words he spoke but studying the nuances of his words and the tone of his voice. His attentive air had not been contrived; he *had been* attentive. He had of course spoken very respectfully to the Director and called him sir.

That was how it was. It was worthwhile to make a good impression on the Director—and dangerous not to. It was important to write reports exactly in the form the Director stipulated. It was essential to adhere strictly to the Director's detailed procedures and standards, set forth in two thick volumes. That was how the man built the unique esprit de corps that had defined the agency.

When the Director sent him to California, Fritz had been unsure if he had been banished for some violation or if he had been rewarded with a plush job. He continued to be troubled by the question until the Director died.

For years now, the vultures had been out to damage the Director's reputation. They said and wrote things about him they wouldn't have *dared* say when he was alive. Now this woman, this Betsy Clendenin, was preparing to do another hatchet job, She actually admitted it, that she was digging up dirt and meant to publish it.

How *could* she? Could *no* one to be spared the indignities of tabloid reporting? The woman was *cheap*; that was plain. She was also persistent. He had no choice but to meet and talk with her, even though he was certain he could not dissuade her from publishing her dirt.

When she called, he would agree to see her. He had no choice. Seeing her might be unpleasant and risky, but God knew what lies she would tell if he didn't.

4

12:37 P.M.

Fritz was disapproving and uneasy as he sat down at a table in Fonda la Paloma. Meeting the woman for lunch committed him to more time than he wanted to give her. He had been led to a table by the window, and he watched the cars turning in, wondering which one would bring Betsy Clendenin. He had a lifelong habit of being everywhere early, so he knew he had time to wait before she would appear—assuming she came on time. He ordered a Beefeater gin on the rocks. He nibbled on taco chips that he dipped in salsa.

Fritz Kloss was in his seventies, of course. He made a point of not allowing himself to gain a pound beyond the weight he'd maintained when he was an agent—and the Director had prescribed lean and neat. His hair had turned white, and he kept it neatly trimmed, never allowing two weeks to pass without a visit to his barber—something else the Director had expected. His face was wrinkled, long, and gaunt. He wore round, silver-rimmed spectacles. Occasionally he allowed himself a variation on the old dress code, and he did today; he was wearing a navy-blue blazer and khaki slacks.

The headwaiter brought the woman to the table. She looked like the whore he thought she was—frosted hair, too much makeup, a knit dress that fit her body too closely, a short skirt showing too much of her stocky legs. It was easy to see why some men would confide in her too readily. Her kind used that influence over gullible men. It was the old, old story, and newshens knew it altogether too well.

'Mr. Kloss. Glad to meet you. I hope you like this place, this kind of food. I come here often. I've done some very good interviews at this table.'

He stood and took her offered hand. 'Miss Clendenin,' he said gravely. He didn't say he was glad to meet her, because he wasn't.

'Well,' she said, pointing at his glass. 'You're ahead of me. Am I late? Glenlivet on the rocks, Eduardo.'

'You're not late,' he said as they sat down. 'I was a few minutes early.'

'Are you ready for Christmas?' she asked.

'I'm afraid I don't celebrate Christmas very much,' he said. 'My wife died many years ago. My children are all grown and live in other parts of the country. I order their gifts from catalogs and have them sent directly. They do the same for me. We'll talk on the telephone. That's about it.'

'I'm alone myself,' she said. 'But I do invite friends to a party I throw the week before Christmas.' She paused, frowned slightly, then

17

smiled. 'As a matter of fact, I'd be pleased if *you* would come to my Christmas party. It will be Monday evening, say eight o'clock. You'll find my friends are interesting people, and I know they'll find you interesting, too.'

Fritz smiled thinly. 'Let's see how our talk goes, Miss Clendenin. We may not like each other very much after this interview.'

Betsy chuckled. 'I try never to be personally offensive. I seek information. Sometimes I do it rather aggressively. But there's nothing personal about it. It's my profession. You've heard of Greg Peters, I suppose. He'll be at the party, in spite of the fact that I did a story about him that he claims cost him a million dollars.'

Fritz sipped gin. 'I'll be frank,' he said. 'You are assaulting the memory of one of the greatest men our country ever produced. A dedicated patriot and a fine gentleman. I'm afraid I tend to resent it, Miss Clendenin. I think you are doing our country a disservice.'

'Fair enough. And *I'll* be frank. I am not going to say anything about J. Edgar Hoover that is not amply supported by evidence. I do not speculate, Mr. Kloss. I report facts. Sometimes I find facts that people do not want exposed. Well—That's too bad. But I don't make up things, and I don't hide what I find out.'

'You never met the Director, I imagine. I mean, you never had the opportunity of

18

talking with him in person.'

'No. I never met Director Hoover.'

'If you had, you could not slander him.' Fritz shook his head. 'You simply could not.'

'I haven't slandered him, Mr. Kloss. I've said and written nothing about him that is not supported by good evidence. And that's the way it's going to be.'

They paused while the headwaiter placed Betsy's drink before her.

'"Good evidence." Gossip?'

'Documentary evidence, Mr. Kloss. From FBI files. From the horse's mouth.'

'Turned over to you? In violation of the law?'

She shrugged. 'Have you heard of the Freedom of Information Act?'

He glowered. 'I've heard of it.'

'And you don't approve of it.'

Fritz nodded. 'No organization, in government or out of it, can do its business if its every private act is subject to being disclosed and to becoming the basis of uninformed analysis and commentary.'

'Shall we talk specifics?' she asked.

The headwaiter remained nearby, probably to know if Fritz wanted another drink. He glanced up, gestured toward his glass, and nodded.

'Mr. Kloss,' said Betsy, 'will you deny that Mr. Hoover was a homosexual?'

'I certainly will,' Fritz said crisply.

'In spite of the overwhelming evidence that proves it?'

'Miss Clendenin,' Fritz sighed. 'It could be 'proved' that George Washington or Abraham Lincoln was a homosexual—using the standards of evidence that your profession accepts. I knew the Director, and I know he was not a homosexual. He was a gentleman in every respect.'

'Alright. There was Clyde Tolson—'

'I knew Mr. Tolson,' Fritz interrupted. 'He was no homosexual.'

'How do you know?'

Fritz shook his head. 'I know a homosexual when I encounter one.'

'Really? Well, how about *me*? Am I a lesbian?'

'Miss Clendenin, I don't know. Mostly because I don't care. If you were a person with whom I had to work, in whom I had to place my trust, I would want to know—and I think I could make the judgment pretty accurately.'

'That's a remarkable talent,' said Betsy dryly. 'It must come in very handy sometimes.'

He shrugged. 'So you think I'm homophobic.'

'No. But tell me, really. What's your judgment of me? Do you think I'm a lesbian?'

'I—Alright, yes. I suspect you are.'

Betsy grinned. 'Why don't you check me out? Surely you have some of the old investigative skills and resources. I'll tell you what you'd find out. You'll find out that I come closer to being a nymphomaniac than a lesbian.'

'I'm not infallible.'

'No. Neither am I. And if you think J. Edgar Hoover was not a compulsive homosexual you're wrong. There's plenty of evidence of it. I don't care about that, really. It's been reported. It's old stuff. You've read, I suppose, about his dressing in women's clothes.'

'That is an outrageous lie,' said Fritz coldly.

'Okay. I didn't write it, and I'm not particularly interested in it. What I'm most interested in at the moment is his relationship with another notorious homosexual—and I don't mean Clyde Tolson.'

'Who do you mean?'

She paused for a moment, then nodded and said, 'I'll omit mention of the *most* notorious. So, what about Roy Cohn?'

'What *about* Roy Cohn?'

'I have information to the effect that material from confidential FBI files was handed over to Roy Cohn.'

'He was on the staff of the Senate investigating committee—the McCarthy committee. Information was given to the Senate, through Cohn.'

'What I'm talking about happened after Senator McCarthy was dead, when Roy Cohn was no longer employed by any agency of the United States government. My information says that Director Hoover turned over confidential files to Cohn in New York, when he was under indictment and was defending himself against criminal charges.'

'That is wholly ridiculous.'

'Can I quote you as saying that it never happened or that it never happened within your knowledge?'

'It never happened, period.'

'You *know* it never happened.'

'I had the honor and privilege of knowing the Director personally, and I can tell you beyond the slightest doubt that he never allowed anyone to have unauthorized access to FBI files—let alone that two-bit felonious shyster Roy Cohn.'

*   *   *

On his way home, Fritz Kloss lit a cigar.

A leak! Goddamnit, there was a leak! Somebody at SOG, or formerly at SOG, had talked to this whore.

Had the Director handed over confidential information to Roy Cohn? Of course he had. For his own good reasons, which Fritz had never seen fit to question. If the Director judged it appropriate to give information to Roy Cohn—or to anyone else, say Carlo Gambino—that was the Director's business.

Six times, he believed it was, Fritz had ridden the Metroliner from Washington to

New York to deliver a locked briefcase to Roy Cohn. He had never asked what was in those briefcases. Each time Cohn had disappeared into another room for a minute or so, then returned with an empty briefcase. He'd made the same little joke two or three times: that the Director would not waste FBI funds by giving away briefcases. Then he'd take Fritz out to lunch or dinner, an expensive lunch or dinner. At one of these dinners, which Fritz vividly remembered, Francis Joseph Cardinal Spellman had joined them. Fritz had wondered at the time if whatever was in the briefcase were not handed over to Cohn for later delivery to the Cardinal. It could have been that the papers in the briefcase had to do with New York City rackets or Communist penetration of New York institutions— information the Cardinal could use in his fights against crime and subversion.

Fritz had had no respect whatever for Cohn but every possible respect for Cardinal Spellman. He doubted the appearance of the Cardinal at dinner had been a coincidence. No, it had been the Director's roundabout way of letting Fritz know who he was working with. Anyway, somebody had leaked to the whore the story of the briefcases carried to New York. God knows what she'd do with it.

He'd accepted the invitation to her party. He needed to know more about her.

23

5

MONDAY, DECEMBER 21—8:49 P.M.

He brought a bottle of champagne to the party. He hoped it was an appropriate gift. Indeed, it seemed to be. The whore accepted it graciously and bore it to a table where she placed it beside other bottles of wine and spirits brought by other guests.

She was wearing a bright red dress with a neckline scooped low and a short, bouffant skirt. If she meant to be a spectacle, she was.

'Here's someone you ought to meet,' she said.

The someone he ought to meet was a woman, fifty years old or so and wearing a gold lamé dress that was too tight for her. Her name was Meredith Nelson, and the whore said she was an actress with a starring role in a daytime serial—in other words, a soap opera.

'I don't think I've ever met a real FBI agent before,' she said.

'I'm not sure I've ever met a real actress before,' said Fritz—and immediately remembered that of course he had; he'd shown houses to actors and actresses, many times. He did not repair the statement. 'I'm afraid I haven't seen your show.'

'To be altogether frank with you, Mr.

Kloss—'

'Fritz,' the whore prompted. 'See that he gets a drink, Meredith.' She moved away to other guests.

'Fritz. To be altogether frank with you, I don't really think I'd care to associate with most of the people who are addicted to our show. That's off the record, of course.'

'One thing that characterizes an FBI agent is the ability to hear confidential things and keep the confidences.'

'I'm sure that must be so. Let's get you a drink.'

Fortunately—fortunately for his purposes—the bar was set up on the kitchen counter. The actress seemed already to have taken him in charge. She poured his drink for him. He glanced around the room and spotted the control panel for the alarm system. Okay. Useful to know.

During the course of the evening he explored the first floor of the house. Her office was just off the living room, a small room equipped with two computers, a ZEOS and a Dell, two filing cabinets, and a shelf of plastic disk caddies filled with floppy disks. On the floor lay two Federal Express boxes, broken open, exposing what he took to be page proofs.

When he had a moment, he asked her. 'I see you work on a computer. Are those your manuscripts on those disks?'

The whore nodded. 'I never print anything out until I'm finished with it. Then I deliver the printout to the publisher. My files are all magnetic.'

'Interesting. I'm not computer-oriented, myself. We had computers in the real-estate office, but I never touched them.'

She smiled. 'The only way to work,' she said.

Meredith Nelson was at his side. She had attached herself to him, and he'd begun to wonder if she expected to leave the party with him. If she did, she had a surprise coming, maybe. He wasn't too old. He could give her a workout.

But he tried for a moment to focus his attention on the house. The whore had a good alarm system. He knew the name and knew how it worked. All of her nasty lies about the Director were on those little computer disks in her office. Okay. Useful things to know. It was why he had come to the party. If he decided to kill the whore, maybe he could destroy her damned manuscripts in the process.

6

WEDNESDAY, DECEMBER 23—2:39 P.M.

A couple of calls, a little plugging around, were enough to locate Harry Lehman. He was where Fritz thought he would be: in Las Vegas. He had to report to a parole officer every month, and that parole officer was a retired agent who knew the name Fritz Kloss, though he had never met him.

On Wednesday afternoon Fritz arrived at the address on Eastern Avenue.

'Mr. Kloss! My *god*!'

'Is that any way to greet an old friend, Harry?'

'Old friend? We're not old friends, Mr. Kloss,' said the diminutive sixty-year-old man with a bald, liver-spotted head and noisy false teeth.

'Bygones are bygones, Harry. Aren't you going to invite me in?'

Lehman stepped back from the door and let Fritz into his modest apartment. He switched off the game show on the television set and gestured toward a dark-green, vinyl-covered recliner chair. Fritz sat down.

'Now that I think of it, I guess you're not here on official business, Mr. Kloss. Sure. You'd of had to retire years ago. I mean, while I was still in the slammer.'

'Right. I retired more than twenty-five years ago, and I'm not here on government business.'

'Well . . . good. The less I see of the government, the better. The government kept me in Leavenworth for twenty-two years, eight months, and seventeen days. That's a hell of a lot of time.'

Fritz nodded grimly. 'You should have

hanged, Harry. You know that as well as I do.'

'If I wasn't, it wasn't because you didn't try. You gave it the ol' college try.'

'That's right. I tried. And I did what I could to keep you in Leavenworth as long as possible.'

'You wrote letters. I never saw 'em, but I was told. You and I aren't friends, Mr. Kloss. Never can be.'

'Maybe. I've kept track of you, Harry. Because you were one of my most interesting cases. I was notified when you were paroled, though I hadn't been an agent for many years. I had some people kind of keep watch on you.'

'Gee, thanks.'

Fritz put his fingers together, in front of his chin. 'What do you know about the federal prison at Marion, Indiana, Harry? The new maximum-security place?'

'Only that it's a tough joint.'

'You could spend the rest of your life there.'

Harry Lehman jerked in a noisy breath. 'Whatta you got in mind?' he whispered hoarsely.

'I told you I kept track of you. If I set hounds on you, they'll figure you out. I have. For instance, what do you live on, Harry?'

Lehman's hands trembled. 'I got a son here. He's got a good job at The Piping Rock Hotel and Casino. He gives me an allowance.'

'That's what you told your parole officer. And in fact your son does give you a check every month. But it's not out of his pockets.

28

He's just passing it through, laundering money so to speak. What you're doing, Harry, is what you used to do, in a smaller way.'

'No! No, you got that wrong. Can't you believe a man can change . . . that the time I did changed me? No, I don't suppose you could. You never give up, huh? Even after you retired. You're still gonna have my ass.'

Fritz smiled faintly and shook his head. 'No, I'm not going to have your ass. Because you and I are going to do each other favors. I'm going to do you one, and you're going to do me one. Two big favors.'

'You makin' some kind of proposition?' Lehinan asked, his eyes narrowing.

Fritz could see the wheels going around in the man's head. Harry was a shrewd old bastard.

'The favor I'm going to do you, Harry, is that I'm going to forget about you. I won't set the hounds on you. You'll see me again in a few days, and then you'll never see or hear from me again.'

'And what am I gonna do for you?'

'I have need of your services.'

'I ain't in that business no more.'

'The hell you're not. That's what I'm telling you: that I can see to it that you go to Marion. Because you're still in the business, just like in the old days. I don't know exactly who your customers are and how much they pay you, but you can bet that the FBI can find out. Or the

29

BATF. They're clever fellows, Harry, and I can help them a lot. I spent a lot of time on you. You put a signature on your work, whether you know it or not. Anyway . . . you'll get your final release from parole in another year, and you'll have enough money to fade out to Acapulco or Rio and live like a king for the rest of your years. You can do that if I don't spoil it for you. And I won't spoil it for you because you're going to do me a favor.'

'Whatta ya want?'

'I want a big bang. I want to kill somebody and blow their whole house to pieces.'

'*You*? You, the goddam angel of the FBI, the Director's fairhaired boy! *You* wanta blow somebody away?'

'Me. I've got a good reason.'

'They always have a good reason. I never knew anybody who wanted to blow somebody away that didn't have a good reason.'

'Well, you've got a good reason. If I don't make a call in the next twenty minutes, you're going to have BATF agents in here looking for chemicals.'

It was a lie, and Harry Lehman was shrewd enough to know it was a lie; but that didn't make any difference.

'What do you have in mind, Mr. Kloss?'

'Your specialty, Harry. RDX.'

'Cyclonite,' said Lehman. 'Cyclo-trimethylenetrinitramine. In a polymeric binder. Plastique. You don't want to send a letter bomb, hmm? You want a *big* son of a bitch.'

'The kind you used to blow away Shondor Birns in Cleveland.'

'I didn't do that job, Mr. Kloss.'

'You made the bomb. The boys in Cleveland knew where to find the expert. You made it, even if you didn't plant it.'

'Mr. Kloss—I never *planted* a bomb in my life. I'm a chemist. Explosions and fires. You want fire? Or just a big old blast?'

'I want a powerful bomb that can be delivered in a package the size of a ream of paper.'

'It doesn't take that much to bring down a 747. Thank god I was in the joint when the plane exploded over Lockerbie. Hey! That one had what you call my signature on it, didn't it, Mr. Kloss?'

'Your signature, Harry. Yeah, your signature. I wondered if it wasn't a student of yours.'

'How do you want to detonate the thing, Mr. Kloss?'

'Not with a timer. I have to have control.'

'Good enough.'

'When can you have it ready, Harry?'

'Well . . . Day after tomorrow is Christmas, after all. My son and his wife will be here, with their children, some of the time. What do you say to Monday?'

'The twenty-eighth. Deal. I'll be earlier than

I was today. I want to drive back to L.A.'

'Stayin' in Vegas tonight?'

'Right.'

'Let me call my son. He can get you a good price on a good room at the Piping Rock.'

7

MONDAY, DECEMBER 28—11:35 A.M.

On December 28 Fritz returned to Harry Lehman's little apartment in Las Vegas.

'It's ready, Mr. Kloss. I see you brought an attaché case. The stuff will fit into that very nicely. With battery and all. Let's look at it.'

The plastic explosive was wrapped in newspaper. Lehman unwrapped it. The material was wrapped in newspaper. It was beige colored, faintly shiny, in the shape of a flat loaf. A blasting cap stuck out of it, with two wires exposed. 'You need a battery. And a control that separates the battery from the cap. Be careful of it, Mr. Kloss. Once the circuit is closed, the cap goes off and the whole schmear goes off. If you make a mistake, they'll have to scrape you off the ceiling—only there won't be any ceiling.'

Fritz nodded. 'I understand. There's enough stuff here to—'

'Blow a car to bits. Bring down an airplane. Or—You mentioned a house. Enough to blow a house to splinters.'

'Very good.'

'Yes. Now, Mr. Kloss. We did not mention my fee. I assume you have brought money.'

'Your fee is that I don't send you to Marion for the rest of your life.'

'Oh, well, you know—'

'I expected this. Pour us a drink, Harry. I favor gin. I do have something for you, in the briefcase.'

Harry Lehman grinned, went to the kitchen, and in a moment returned with a glass of gin on the rocks. 'I don't use the stuff anymore,' he said. 'Twenty-two years without it, you learn to live without it. I figure I'll live longer.'

Fritz raised the glass and took a sip of the gin. He snapped open the catches on the briefcase and raised the lid toward Lehman, who could not see what was inside. What was inside was a nine-millimeter Beretta equipped with a silencer. Fritz smiled faintly as he raised the pistol and fired two quick shots into Lehman's chest. When the man was down he finished him with a shot to the head.

He finished the gin and put the glass—the only thing in the apartment with his fingerprints on it—in the attaché case. Then he put in the bomb. He snapped the case shut and shoved the pistol down into the waistband of his pants, under his suit jacket. He wrapped his hand in a handkerchief and opened the door.

TUESDAY, DECEMBER 29—7:28 A.M.

In the garage of his house on Las Virgence Road, Fritz climbed a ladder toward the ceiling. Using a screwdriver and pliers, he took the case off one of the two garage-door openers—the one that opened the right-hand door, the side of the garage where his late wife had parked her car. This opener had been disconnected for years, so he wouldn't open both doors every time he pressed the button on his controller. He had reconnected it this morning, to see if it still worked. It did.

He removed the innards from it and took them down. He replaced the case.

The opener was a simple mechanism. When the little radio receiver detected a signal from the controller, it closed a switch that sent current to the electric motor that raised the door. That switch could just as readily send current to the detonator in the bomb.

The only problem was to find power for the receiver. That problem was easily enough solved for anyone who knew anything about electronics. The unit was powered by the 110 house current—which, however, was first reduced by a transformer to twelve volts, then run through a rectifier to change the alternating current to direct current. All Fritz had to do was apply the probes of a multimeter to the connections to find the point

34

where the receiver took in its direct current. Sending in battery current right there activated the receiver. In fact, the battery that would explode the detonator could also power the receiver.

He worked most of the day, soldering connections, testing, testing, testing. When he was satisfied, he could press the button on the garage-door controller and watch the needle shoot across the face of the multimeter, one hundred percent reliably. It had to be that way: one-hundred-percent reliable.

So far, so good.

WEDNESDAY, DECEMBER 30— 11:42 A.M.

On Wednesday he took the transmitter to West Santa Monica Boulevard, parked across the street from the whore's house, and pressed the button.

Her door did not open. Good. Her garage-door opener operated on a different frequency. She would not detonate his bomb when she opened her garage door.

But—Uh-oh. A garage door down the street went up. What if the neighbor used his transmitter to open his garage door when the bomb was waiting for the whore?

He had a cure for the problem. The antenna on a garage-door opener, this vintage, consisted of a piece of wire. With a long

35

antenna, the door would open if the transmitter sent a signal from a hundred yards away. With a shorter antenna, it would open the door only if the signal came from a hundred feet away. When he had first bought a radio-controlled garage-door opener, he had stretched an antenna so long that he could open his door from the moment he pulled into his street. Later, having learned that the long antenna would pick up a lot of stray signals, he cut the antenna short.

He experimented with this one. He didn't want the whore's neighbor detonating his bomb. He adjusted the antenna on the bomb to receive signals from two hundred feet—far enough away to put him beyond the range of the blast, too far away for the neighbor's opener to set off the bomb.

In the afternoon he stopped by a FedEx office and picked up a box and an airbill.

8

NEW YEAR'S EVE—7:19 P.M.

New Year's Eve. He'd bet the whore was going to go out and get drunk, maybe laid. He himself had accepted an invitation from Meredith Nelson to go to a New Year's Eve party. The party began at nine, and he'd told her he'd pick her up at her house at eight-thirty.

The call from Meredith had not been entirely a surprise. Fritz prided himself on still being attractive to women, in his seventies. He had not bedded her the night of the whore's party, but he could be sure he would tonight. He had pretended he was greatly pleased to hear from her, thanked her for the invitation, and bought a bottle of champagne for her which he hoped they would open in her apartment sometime after midnight, after they had celebrated the New Year at the party.

After sunset—which was of course very early at that time of year—he drove to the whore's house on West Santa Monica Boulevard.

Luck was with him. Of course it didn't have to be: he could come back as often as necessary. But it was with him tonight. The house was dark except for the lights she always left on. The whore was not home.

He parked at a distance down the street. He left his car and carried the bomb to her doorstep. It was in the distinctive box of Federal Express, and he had slipped into the transparent envelope attached the recipient's copy of an airbill saying that the package came from a New York publisher.

He went back to his car and sat down to wait.

The whore arrived about 7:30. Fritz left his car and walked closer.

She switched on lights and drove into her

garage. All but certainly she had noticed the FedEx package on her doorstep.

He watched the lights coming on inside. She opened the front door and picked up the FedEx package. Fritz waited for her to carry it well inside the house—with any luck, into her office. He was patient. He waited, watching for the light to come on in the room off the living room, her office. She had been inside the house maybe four minutes before he saw that light come on. Only then did he press the button.

The controller sent a radio signal to the receiver. The receiver closed the switch that sent a current to the detonator cap. A shock wave blew out the walls of the house, sent the upper floor and the roof into the air, and collapsed walls of the two houses adjoining.

Fritz could not smile. He stared and nodded. The whore was dead. With any luck, her slanderous computer disks had been destroyed.

NEW YEAR'S EVE—8:34 P.M.

When he arrived at Meredith Nelson's house to take her to the party, she asked him if he was really all that interested in the New Year's Eve party, or would he rather stay here and have their own party. He wasn't entirely surprised and readily agreed.

She'd known he would. She had hors

38

d'oeuvres laid out on a tray, bottles set out, ice in a bucket, and a bottle of champagne for midnight. But when he tried to kiss her, she ducked away. First she wanted a promise. She wanted him to promise he would not leave but would stay all night, would stay in fact long enough to watch the parades on New Year's Day. He promised. She took him by the arm and led him straight to her bedroom. She was no girl; she was a strapping big voluptuous woman; and she brought a straightforward approach to what they were going to do—no feigned naiveté, no coyness, no kidding around.

After half an hour or so she got up and went to pour them fresh drinks. 'Well,' she said when she returned, 'how about staying for the football games, lover?'

'Hell, I'll stay for the World Series.'

She chuckled. 'Let's see what's on the tube.' She began to press buttons on the clicker.

Fritz went in the bathroom and was there several minutes.

'*Fritz!*'

'What?'

'*Jesus H. Christ!* Looka this!'

'Looka wha'?'

'My *god! Betsy*'s been murdered! Betsy Clendenin! Looka! Looka! Somebody blew her away!'

Fritz shook his head as he stared at the television image of the shattered houses on

39

West Santa Monica Boulevard. 'Well, I . . . I guess you gotta figure a number of people might want to do that.'

'Yeah, well—Somebody's gonna wish they didn't.'

'Huh?'

'Look who's on the job!'

'Whatta you mean?'

'That guy there. That guy in the raincoat. That's Lieutenant Columbo, LAPD. He never misses. He'll get whoever did it. If I was the guy that blew up Betsy, I'd be shakin' in my shoes.'

PART TWO

'Thank you, Lieutenant Columbo, but I'm afraid my job is just to stay out here and keep people from ducking under the tape.'

'I s'pose. Well, whatever the lord gives you to do, do it with all your might—or somethin' like that—whatever it is they say.'

'One of those new guys that just graduated from the FBI Academy is a pinhead! Get rid of him!'

—JOHN EDGAR HOOVER

9

NEW YEAR'S EVE—9:01 P.M.

In all his years as a policeman, Columbo had never seen anything like what he saw when he turned into the block on West Santa Monica Boulevard. The fire department was still spraying water onto tangled debris that was not even recognizable as the ruins of a house. They had spread huge tarpaulins over the broken walls of the adjoining houses and were keeping the roofs and tarps wet. The heaped debris and the two adjoining houses were lighted by glaring floodlights. Otherwise, everything was dark; the electricity had been switched off for the whole block.

Red and blue strobe lights flashed on fire, police, and medical vehicles. Crisp voices crackled on radios, piercing the rumble of the diesel engines that powered the fire-engine pumps and the generators that supplied power for the floodlights.

He knew all the activity was purposeful and organized, but Columbo could see no organization or purpose; everyone seemed to be scurrying at random, all over the place.

'Y'can't leave that car there, Mac.'

'B'lieve I can,' he said to the young uniformed officer who strode purposefully toward him. 'Columbo. LAPD Homicide.'

'Yeah? Well, let me see some ID.'

Columbo shifted his cigar from his hand to his mouth and reached inside his jacket. 'There y' go,' he said, thrusting under the cop's nose his shield and photo ID card.

The young patrolman was not much impressed. 'Okay,' he said grudgingly. 'But I suppose you'll agree, you don't look like a police detective, Lieutenant.'

Columbo pulled the cigar from his mouth. 'That may be the secret of my success, son,' he said.

The young policeman frowned. 'I suggest you wear your shield on your raincoat, Sir,' he said. 'Lot of nervous people around here.'

'Most of them know me. Who's in charge?'

'Lieutenant Lawrence, the watch commander.'

Columbo shook his head. 'Pat's gonna love it that this one came up on *his* tour.'

'The detective in charge right now is Sergeant Zimmer, Sir.'

'Martha. She's a fine detective. You keep an eye on how *she* works, and you'll see how it's done.'

'Thank you, Lieutenant Columbo, but I'm afraid my job is just to stay out here and keep people from ducking under the yellow tape.'

'I s'pose. Well, whatever the lord gives you to do, do it with all your might—or somethin' like that—whatever it is they say. Wanta lift that tape for me?'

He spotted Martha Zimmer. She was on the street, not inside the house. There *wasn't* any house.

'I tried to get you out of this one, Columbo,' she said.

'Yeah. Mrs. Columbo's awful ticked. We've got people comin' for a party tonight. She's bought paper hats and all that jazz, an'—Well, I gotta take a look at this and get home. Sure gotta be there before midnight.'

'It's another celebrity case, Columbo. That's why Captain Sczciegel insisted it had to be you.'

Columbo looked at his cigar. It had gone out. He pinched it a little to be sure there was no fire in it, then dropped it in his raincoat pocket. 'What's the story, Martha?'

Martha Zimmer was a very professional detective. She reached into a pocket of her navy-blue blazer and pulled out a small notebook. She *was* professional, though she looked like anything but a detective and had to carry her badge in a leather holder that folded out of her breast pocket, so people would see it and understand she was an officer of LAPD. She was short and heavy, the mother of three children and pregnant with a fourth. Her dark hair was curly and short, and she had pudgy apple cheeks. Columbo had worked with her often and had a lot of respect for her. They were friends, too. She had confided to him

45

that she was pregnant again, though she didn't want the Department to know it yet.

'Okay. The woman who lived here was named Betsy Clendenin. She was a professional writer, specialized in juicy exposés. About seven-thirty—'

'Was she home when—?'

'Afraid so. Anyway, *somebody* was home, *some* woman.'

'I'm afraid to ask.'

Martha pointed to a small square of plastic lying on the street pavement, covering something, guarded by a uniformed policewoman. 'That's her head, Columbo. I haven't looked at it. The guys who have are feeling kinda sick.'

'Was anyone else hurt?'

'No. Fortunately, the people in the houses on both sides had gone out to parties. There's not a window within two hundred yards in all directions that's not broken, but nobody was hit by flying glass.'

Columbo walked toward the wreckage. 'Crime Scene?' he asked.

'Jean Pavlov's here.'

'Oh, yeah.' He walked over to an attractive young woman in a sweatshirt and blue jeans, wearing her shield on the sweatshirt. She was a technician with the Crime Scene Unit. He had worked with her before. 'Hiya, Pavlov. Got ya workin' on New Year's Eve, I see.'

'My regular tour,' she said. 'I got Christmas

off.'

'Whatta ya figure here?'

'One hell of a bomb, Lieutenant. Cyclonite, I'd guess. The lab tests will tell us for sure.'

'Couldn't be a gas explosion?'

'The house was heated with oil.'

'The body?'

'We may never find all of it,' she said. 'The trunk is mangled but essentially intact. Odd thing about explosions. Sometimes the worst damage doesn't happen right at the center, so we've got a crushed but intact trunk. It's in a body bag in the ambulance, incidentally. The fire guys brought it out so it wouldn't get burned. The head's out there on the street. We're leaving it till we can get an exact measurement of its position and get some photos. Arms and legs—' She shrugged.

'I don't hafta tell ya it'd be great to find out how the bomb was set off. Any chance at all?'

'Good chance. What we've got to do is sift this debris like we were sifting sand for gold. I wouldn't be surprised if we find enough to tell us what kind of detonator was used.'

'Spraying all that water isn't preserving the evidence,' said Columbo, glancing at the firemen whose nozzles were set to drench the debris with spray, not to shoot streams at it. 'When I got here there was still a lot of flame,' said Jean Pavlov. 'The oil tank ruptured, and the heating oil caught fire.'

'It looks to me,' said Columbo, 'like there

47

isn't much for me to do here tonight. This has gotta be a *scientific* investigation.'

'We can't even get in there and begin to sift,' said Jean, 'until the fire guys are sure the fire is out and stop their damn spraying.'

'Thanks, Pavlov. I'll be talkin' to ya again, I expect.'

Columbo went to the watch commander, Lieutenant Patrick Lawrence. 'Hiya, Pat. Ever see anything like this before?'

The watch commander was everyone's picture of the perfect policeman: tall and erect, with intent blue eyes, wearing a crisply pressed uniform. 'I never did, Lieutenant Columbo,' he said grimly.

'Y'started inquiries in the neighborhood?'

'A little. One family is away somewhere and doesn't even know yet that their house has been damaged. Sergeant Zimmer over there is talking to Mr. Agon. He lives three doors down.'

'I'll see what he's telling her.'

Martha Zimmer introduced Columbo to Edmund Agon, a balding, middle-aged man. 'Mr. Agon has lost all his windows, and a piece of debris landed on his roof.'

'Insurance will take care of me,' said Agon. 'But *Jesus Christ*!'

'Ya know the woman?' Columbo asked.

'To speak to, that's all. She seemed like a pleasant enough person.'

'I guess you've been asked the usual

48

questions, like did ya see anybody strange around the neighborhood, and all.'

'My wife and I didn't see a thing. We were getting ready to go out. Suddenly—' Agon threw out his hands. 'During the Gulf War I heard a Scud missile land—' He shook his head. 'It was like that. By the time I got outside and could look, I saw a car going around the corner up there. It was too far away for me to get any kind of a fix on it. Anyway, I wasn't looking at it. Lieutenant Columbo . . . I saw her head lying out there on the street.'

'Well, thank ya, Mr. Agon. I'll leave you with Sergeant Zimmer. I—Oh. One little thing. Is that your house, with the garage door open?'

'Right. And maybe that's odd, Lieutenant. We didn't open that door. It just opened. It happened yesterday, too. I came home and found my garage door up.'

'Make a note of that,' Columbo said to Martha. 'And make sure Pavlov knows about it. Thank ya again, Mr. Agon. I think you just told us somethin' very useful.'

10

NEW YEAR'S DAY—9:19 A.M.

New Year's Day. A glum smog hung over Los Angeles, and the scene on West Santa Monica

Boulevard was grimmer than it had been last night. One red pumper remained on the street, but the firemen had rolled up all but one of their hoses and were just keeping watch. The block was still closed by black-and-whites parked across the street at both ends. Two other units were at the house, also three unmarked cars with emergency lights stuck on by magnets. A Crime Scene Unit van was parked in front of the house.

Columbo frowned and stared and was glad to see the woman's head no longer lay on the street. He stopped the Peugeot at the yellow tape that was stretched across the street. 'Hiya, Ramirez,' he said, reading the uniformed officer's name off his tag. 'Columbo, Homicide.'

'Yes, Sir. I recognize you.'

'No holiday for us guys, huh?'

'Well, at least I got to stay home last night,' said Ramirez. 'I saw *you* on television.'

'I wasn't here long. This is a job for Crime Scene, right now. I got home for the party my wife had, most of it. I may get home for the football games. Hey, kinda keep an eye on my car, will ya? It's got a lotta miles on it, and I wouldn't want anything to happen to it.'

Ramirez stared skeptically at the aged Peugeot, sitting sort of squat on the street, as if its wheels were in danger of buckling outward and dropping the chassis on the pavement. 'I'll lift the tape, Lieutenant. Then you can drive it into the closed area with the rest of the official cars.'

'Thank ya, Ramirez. I'll—'

'Hey, Columbo!'

It was Adrienne Boswell. She was climbing out of her shiny new red Alfa Romeo.

'The lady wants to enter the area, Lieutenant,' said Ramirez.

'She's a reporter,' Columbo explained.

Adrienne strode toward her. She tossed her head as she came, to flip her flaming-red hair off her face. She was always stylish, always handsome in no matter what she wore; and this morning she was stunning in nothing but a pair of tight, well-faded blue jeans and a red sweatshirt.

I saw you on the tube last night,' she said. 'Figured you'd show up here this morning. Hey! Take me in with you. This is the story of the new year.'

'That'd be a little tough to do, Adrienne. The area is closed. If I take you in, it'd look like I got a pet reporter.'

'Closed? Pet reporter? Whatta you call those television cameras and the people working them? It's not Ramirez's fault, but somebody's got the signals crossed.'

Ramirez shrugged. 'Your call, Lieutenant,' he said. 'You outrank the guy who gave me the orders.'

'Well, I'll take the lady in with me. My responsibility.'

51

Columbo and Adrienne walked toward the debris of the Clendenin home.

'Thought you'd take the day off,' Columbo said.

'Dan's mad as hell,' she said. 'But this is a *story*, Columbo. This is a story. Dan will be there when I get home.'

'Yeah. So will Mrs. C when I get home. But I wish I didn't hafta—'

'You hafta. I hafta. I figured out something about you a long time ago, Columbo. Your work is your life. Well . . . so's mine.'

'You know the lady? I mean, the deceased.'

I knew her well,' Adrienne said sadly. 'Hell—This could've happened to *me*.'

'So who did it? Y'got any ideas?'

'Well—That book she did on Jonathan ruined him. She got threats while she was working on it, warning her not to publish. And she got threats afterward. Jonathan is not capable of killing anybody, particularly this way. But he was a valuable asset to some people who are.'

'There are others?'

'You bet. She told the truth about people, Columbo. She wasn't quite as careful about it as I try to be. She accepted as evidence some things I wouldn't accept. But she never lost a libel suit. If you want a suggestion from me, look into the people she exposed.'

'I gotta kind of different idea,' Columbo said. 'I kinda figure this is a hard way to go just to get revenge. I'd like to know what was *coming*, what she was working on.'

'You ought to read *Glitz*. Having put Ai-ling Cooper away for ten years, the least you could do is read her magazine. Or watch tabloid TV. You'd know what she was working on.'

'What?'

'An exposé of J. Edgar Hoover.'

'Well, it's for sure he didn't kill her.'

I'd like to know what else she was working on,' said Adrienne, 'but what you want to bet her files were in the house?'

*   *   *

The Crime Scene Unit had driven stakes in the ground all around the debris and had run white cords from stake to stake, to form a grid of squares. Men and women were working gingerly in the grid, finding bits of what might be evidence, photographing it in place, then placing the bits in bags and boxes marked with the coordinates of the grid, to show where each piece was found.

Columbo told Adrienne she could not go with him to the grid and the collection of evidence. She went to the pumper and began to interview the firemen.

'Hiya, Pavlov. You been here all this time?'

Jean Pavlov shook her head. 'I went home and came back,' she said. 'Had a bath, a little sleep, a change of clothes.'

'Findin' a lot of stuff?'

She rubbed her hand on her sweatshirt and then wiped her eyes. 'Yeah. Some things we wish we hadn't. We've found some pieces of the victim. Two fingers. Part of a foot. Let me show you some other things.'

Boxes were laid out on the lawn. She put on rubber gloves and picked up a shred of metal. It was torn and twisted, exposing bright steel, but part of it was covered with a metallic gray enamel.

'We don't know what that is for sure,' said Jean, 'but when you sent word last night that a neighbor's garage door went up, we started looking for pieces of a garage-door opener. That could be the steel case of an opener. And we've got something else—'

She picked up from another box a fragment of vinyl. One side of it was marked with a pattern of silvery lines. Two tiny cylinders that Columbo recognized as resistors clung to the fragment.

'Piece of a circuit board,' she said.

'Could be a piece out of her computer.'

'Look closer.'

'I don't know much about these technological things. What am I supposed to be seein', Pavlov?'

'Look how thick that board is. You don't see that in a computer manufactured in the last ten or twenty years. I can be wrong, and the lab guys will check it out; but I'd guess that circuit board is older than any computer she had in the house.'

'Meanin' garage-door opener?'

'Meaning *old* garage-door opener.'

'Meaning the guy that set off the explosion took down the opener off his own garage,' said Columbo. 'Good. All we gotta do is find a garage with an opener that was taken down.'

Jean Pavlov shrugged. 'We do the best we can.'

'An' ya do very well, Jean. I sure don't mean to put ya down.'

'Show you something else,' she said. 'Look over here. These are fragments of a Federal Express carton—or maybe several FedEx cartons. I think several. Notice how most of these pieces are the size of a playing card or bigger. Then we've got these pieces that are the size of a postage stamp. Speculation, Columbo. The little pieces are fragments of a carton the bomb came in.'

'They could survive like that?'

She nodded. 'Only a few of them. Explosives don't vaporize things, generally. Just rip them to pieces. We've got work to do. The bigger pieces may fit together and make, like, the ruins of a carton—some pieces missing. The little pieces aren't going to fit together. Maybe they come from another carton.'

'You'll be at it all day, huh?'

'And all night. Another tour will come on. Sifting, sifting. God save me we don't find more fingers and toes.'

11

SATURDAY, JANUARY 2—11:39 A.M.

'This one ya don't have to show me, Doc. This one I don't want to see.'

Columbo was talking to Dr. Harold Culp, the medical examiner, on Saturday, the day after New Year's.

'In that case,' said Dr. Culp, 'let's go to lunch. I was just about to go out.'

'Hey! I can introduce you to the best chili in town! I got a place where—'

The doctor smiled and shook his head. 'I've heard about Burt's chili. I understand its harder on the stomach than doing a messy autopsy. No, thanks, Columbo. You ever eat at Drake's Sandwich Shop?'

'How 'bout fish 'n' chips?' Columbo asked. 'I do like seafood.'

Ten minutes later they were seated in a booth in Bow Bells Fish 'n' Chips. Columbo's raincoat hung on the hook beside him, one pocket bulging with the two hard-boiled eggs he had carried from home that morning and had not found time to eat. He had two cellophane-wrapped cigars in the breast pocket of his jacket, plus a half-burned stub in a raincoat pocket. (He was always careful not to put unwrapped cigars in the same pocket

56

with eggs.) As usual, the narrow end of his necktie hung below the wide end.

'I guess I know what killed the lady. You find anything unusual? I mean, you find anything you didn't expect?'

Dr. Culp shook his head. 'The usual thing. She was literally torn to pieces, died instantly. I picked a lot of junk out of the trunk of her body and turned it over to the crime lab. There were some bits of steel, like shrapnel. Also, some hunks of brown plastic with etching on them, which I took for hunks of a circuit board. I picked out some shreds of some kind of heavy paper, or paperboard. It was soaked with blood, so I couldn't tell much about it, but some pieces seemed to have been printed blue and some red.'

'Bits of a FedEx box?' Columbo asked.

Dr. Culp ran his hand over the cup-sized bald spot on the back of his head as he thought for a moment, then nodded. 'Could be.'

'We pretty well know how the bomb was delivered and how it was detonated.'

They paused while a waitress put their lunches in front of them—generous servings of fried white fish with what Americans called French fries, also large paper cups of Pepsi. 'What I call lunch,' Columbo observed after the waitress was gone. 'I mean, second to Burt's chili. I'm a guy with simple tastes, ya know? Once in a while I hafta eat in fancy places, but for everyday this suits me just fine.'

'I'm that kind of guy myself,' said Dr. Culp. 'I can't take a lot of time for lunch. Some people wonder how I can eat lunch at all, considering what I do in the morning.'

'I won't go into that,' said Columbo.

'Getting back to the body of Betsy Clendenin, you might be interested in what I *didn't* find—which is the remains of her clothes. I didn't find a shred of any kind of fabric. Or a button, or a piece of zipper, or anything. If that other junk was driven into her flesh by the explosion, her clothes would have been, too. Conclusion: When the lady died, she was stark, staring naked. Isn't that kind of interesting?'

Columbo frowned. 'Could you tell if she'd had sex just before she died?'

Dr. Culp turned down the corners of his mouth and shook his head. 'No way to tell. Not enough left of her to tell. I couldn't even find the contents of her stomach and intestines. They had been torn open, and whatever was in them went flying. It might have been on the floor, but I'm told the fire department had to spray water all over. In fact, their spray had washed all the blood off of her.'

Columbo poured malt vinegar over his fish. 'Interesting as usual, Doctor,' he said. 'What did you think of the Rose Bowl game?'

'Hiya, Mulhaney,' said Columbo as he walked into the police laboratory.

Tim Mulhaney, a tall, solemn young man, wearing round, plastic-rimmed eyeglasses, with hair neatly trimmed and clothes pressed and brushed, was the product of a special program established by LAPD to attract young university graduates to police work. He held the rank of detective and often went out on investigations, but he spent most of the time in the lab. He had attended many seminars and conferences on forensic science. Lately he had begun teaching seminars.

'Good afternoon, Lieutenant. Come on in my office and have a seat.'

Mulhaney's office was a cubicle. It was crowded with books on gray steel shelves. A long white lab coat was draped over the visitor's chair, and he picked it up and hung it over the top of the cubicle.

'I don't think I can tell you anything you don't know,' he said to Columbo. 'Mostly, what I can do is confirm what Jean Pavlov told you or surmised. There may be some other information next week. We're turning some explosives residue over to the Bureau of Alcohol, Tobacco and Firearms, for laboratory analysis.'

'Whatta ya figure those guys can tell us?' Columbo asked. 'I mean, that you don't

59

already know.'

'Well, I can tell you that the explosive was RDX, cyclonite, but I want to know what the binder was. When you know that, you can sometimes tell who made the bomb. Different people make plastic explosives different ways.'

'What about the circuit board?'

'Jean had that one figured out,' said Mulhaney. 'That circuit board came out of a device manufactured at least ten years ago, and I'd think more like twenty. They don't make em like that anymore: thick and brown.'

'Garage-door opener?'

'Could be. That would send and receive a strong signal. The switch in it, tripped by the radio signal, would very well close the circuit between the battery and the detonator.'

'There's a man down the street by the name of Agon,' said Columbo. 'His garage door went up about the same time as the explosion. I'd appreciate it if you'd check that opener and see what frequency it operates on.'

'Had a note to do just that,' said Mulhaney.

'So. We got a pretty good idea what kind of bomb it was and how it was set off. All we need to do now is figure out who did it.'

12

That afternoon Columbo went to a men's clothing store. He stood on the street outside Pittocco's, studying the clothing displayed in the window. He had to go in; there was nothing else for it. For Christmas, Mrs. C had given him a gift certificate, so he had to go in here; he had to use it.

Why couldn't she have given him a gift certificate in a less swanky place, like a nice outlet store? He dreaded the clerk who would try to sell him something. He absolutely dreaded it. Those guys—

Well. He took a final puff from his cigar, tossed the stub into the gutter, and pulled open a big glass door.

'Good afternoon, Sir. How can we help you?'

It wasn't a guy. That is, *she* wasn't a guy. She was a woman and a damn good-looking woman, too: probably in her forties, as he judged, dark-haired, dark-eyed, wearing a form-hugging but modest gray wool dress.

'Well, uh, my wife . . . gave me a gift certificate, for Christmas. She wants me to get a new raincoat.'

'Yes. We have some very nice ones. Right over here.'

He followed her to a rack where a score of raincoats were on display.

'Would you like to take off your raincoat so you can try one on?'

'Uh . . . Okay, I guess. Uh, y'see, I guess I oughta explain somethin'. What I do for a living, I'm a policeman. That is, I'm a detective, LAPD Homicide.'

'You're Lieutenant Columbo. I thought I recognized you.'

'Right. I guess I show up on television more than I wish I did.'

'I saw you on Court TV when you testified in the Grant Kellog and Erika Björling case.'

'That was a tough one.'

'I gathered you felt sorry for Erika Björling.'

'He'd exploited her,' said Columbo.

'Anyway, let me show you the best raincoat we have. It's a Burberrys, imported from England.'

Reluctantly, Columbo slipped into the English raincoat. He thought he looked idiotic in it. In the first place, it was *long*, reaching almost to his ankles. Besides, it was doublebreasted, and it had a belt.

'It's really handsome. You'll want a size smaller, of course.'

'Yeah, well . . . let me explain somethin', Ma'am. Look at that coat I came in wearin'. See what I've done to it? I crawl around in the dirt sometimes. Lookin' for things, y' know. And I keep all kinds of things in the pockets. Cigars half burned. Hard-boiled eggs. Bullets sometimes. Notebook, if I remember to carry one. Anyway, this has got a belt, and the first thing I'd do would be lose the belt. I'm awful about things like that.'

'The belt on a Burberrys is tied in back and rarely if ever used. That's the style. We can tie it for you, and you'll never need to think about it. Let me get you one of the right size.'

The woman disappeared through a door. Columbo stared at himself in the mirror. No matter what she said, he felt foolish. He didn't see how he could show up at the office wearing a raincoat halfway down to his ankles. With all these straps and loops.

Then he looked at the price. My god! He shrugged out of the coat and draped it carefully over a rack of slacks.

'This one will fit, Lieutenant Columbo, and we'll tie the belt so—'

'Ma'am, I appreciate it, but I think I'd better look at some other way to use my gift certificate. Y' know, that raincoat there has given me awful good service for many years. I guess I'm sort of attached to it, too. I do hate to give up somethin' that's given me good service. Makes me sort of feel like I'm *betrayin'* the thing. Like, I got a car that—Well . . .'

The elegant woman nodded. 'I have a pair of shoes like that. They're so comfortable. They're really worn out, but I just can't bear to give them up.'

'Maybe you could show me a jacket.'

'Of course. Right back here. We fit police people from time to time. Are you carrying your sidearm? We'll tailor the jacket to fit over it.'

'Well, no, Ma'am. I—'

'No matter. The tailor has a shoulder holster with a block of wood in it. He can fit

63

your jacket so your pistol won't make a bulge.'

When he left the store forty-five minutes later, he had bought a plaid wool jacket in shades of brown, plus a necktie the woman had insisted he must have to wear with it. He had not realized a man could spend fifty dollars on a necktie and resolved to be very careful tying it, so as to get the wide end below the narrow end. He had exceeded the amount of his gift certificate and had to offer a VISA card to cover the balance. Mrs. Columbo would be distressed to see the old raincoat, which she had told him to leave in the trash at the store, but she'd be pleased with his nifty new jacket. All he was carrying home was the tie in a box. The jacket wouldn't be ready for a week.

13

MONDAY, JANUARY 4—8:49 A.M.

On Monday morning Columbo went to the office. He found on his desk a report from a junior detective who had been interviewing the residents of West Santa Monica Boulevard—

Mrs. Barbara Fitzmeyer indicates that she observed a man standing across and west on the street from the Clendenin home during the few minutes preceding the explosion. She describes him as a man of somewhat more than average height, well-dressed, wearing a hat. She paid no particular attention to him, since he impressed her as the kind of man who lived in that neighborhood or might be visiting it. The light on the street was quite dim, so she can give no further details on the man's appearance. She indicates that a car was parked farther west, but she did not notice anything about it.

'Likely our guy,' Columbo said to Martha Zimmer, handing her the report. She had come to his desk as he read it. 'Goes to show, ya can't count on bein' anywhere that somebody won't notice ya.'

'Not much help,' said Martha as she handed the report back.

'No. Better than nothing, but not much better.'

'Where do we start, Columbo?'

'Me, I'm gonna start with Jonathan.'

2:20 P.M.

Jonathan called his estate Xanadu. It consisted of 340 acres, surrounded by a high fence topped with coils of razor wire. Behind the razor wire lay an unpaved road, patrolled day and night by white Jeeps carrying armed guards. Sensors scanned the grounds, watching for movement, heat, and magnetic radiation, listening for sound. Doberman pinschers roamed the acres.

The house was nothing as grand as the Hearst estate at San Simeon, but it was in that category: a grandiose palace, a basilica built to the glory of a billion-dollar star. A miniature, steam-powered railroad ran around the estate. A hundred yards from the house were a landing strip and helicopter landing pad. Steel barriers on strip and pad prevented the landing of unauthorized aircraft. Dish antennas on the roof of one wing of the house received television signals from all over the world and served as antennae for an elaborate communications system.

Except for the television dish, the antennae were dead now. Xanadu was no longer the focus of a worldwide entertainment enterprise.

Columbo drove up to the main gate. No one came out. He honked his horn.

No one came out. A speaker blared. 'No one admitted. Turn around and go! You're trespassing.'

'Don't really think so,' Columbo yelled. 'I'm Lieutenant Columbo, LAPD Homicide.'

'Hold on a minute.'

Columbo leaned against the Peugeot and lit a cigar. A door opened in the gatehouse, and a man came out.

The man: beefy, brush-cut, florid, wearing a light-blue faux police uniform, stared skeptically at Columbo. Columbo showed his identification.

'You're outside your jurisdiction.'

'Yeah. But if Mr. Jonathan doesn't talk to me now, he's gonna hafta talk to me at the sheriff's office a little later. Up to him.'

'You think you can make that stick, Lieutenant?'

'I can make it stick. Might have been tough a year ago, but the woman who was blown up last Thursday evening changed all that forever. Your boss doesn't run the world to suit him anymore. The way I hear it, there's a limit to what money and celebrity can buy, an' Miz Betsy Clendenin showed Mr. Jonathan where that limit is.'

'So whatta ya want?'

'All I wanta do is ask a few questions.'

'Lemme make a call.'

A minute later Columbo drove the Peugeot through the gate and toward the house, led by a white Jeep he was told to follow. At the main entrance to the house, the driver of the Jeep— another bruiser in a light-blue uniform— pointed to a parking space under a tree. Columbo parked his car. A houseman opened the door and beckoned Columbo to come in.

'My, this is some elegant place that Mr. Jonathan has!'

'He is not *Mr.* Jonathan, Sir. Jonathan is his Christian name. He does not use his family name. You are quite welcome to call him

Jonathan. Everyone does.'

The houseman led Columbo through the house. Columbo reflected that it was not elegant, really; it was flamboyant, flashy, pretentious . . . not elegant. The marble and gilding were cold. The hall through which he was led toward the back of the house was like a corridor in an ostentatiously sumptuous hotel. The swimming pool, paved in mosaics representing Neptune frolicking with naiads, was an acre in expanse but never more than four feet deep. It lay in an artificial grotto of concrete cast to look like stone, with lush plantings all around. Six *real* naiads, girls not yet nubile and all ingenuously naked, romped gaily in the water for the amusement of the man the world knew as Jonathan.

Columbo had seen many pictures and had known what to expect. Though for years no one had used the word, the truth was that Jonathan was an albino. His hair was white, and his skin was white: *unnaturally* white. He sat in a chaise longue, in the shade of a huge umbrella, wearing a red thong bikini bottom and a Dodgers baseball cap. As Columbo approached he removed his sunglasses, perhaps to see the detective better, maybe to let him have a moment's view of his pinkish pale-blue eyes.

On the stage, under colored lights, wearing his trademark makeup of black lipstick, black eyeshadow and eyeliner, Jonathan was a spectacular figure, or monstrous, depending on one's point of view. Millions of devoted fans had all but canonized him. Many other millions loathed him. Disclosures by Betsy Clendenin had changed the mix. The number of worshipful fans was much diminished, and a record by Jonathan was no longer a guaranteed platinum.

'Lieutenant Columbo,' he said. His conversational voice was like his singing voice: high-pitched and smooth and smarmy. 'I've heard of you. Sit down. Let Charles have your raincoat. In fact, if you'd like to take a dip in the pool, we have cabanas where—'

'Well, no thank ya, Sir. I won't be stayin' long. I just came by to ask one or two short questions.'

'Have a drink at least.'

'I'm on duty, but I guess a light Scotch wouldn't hurt. Y' got a luxurious place here. I never saw anything quite like it.'

'Nobody ever *did*, Lieutenant,' said Jonathan with a languid smile. He put on his sunglasses again. 'Do you like my nymphs? The people sitting on the other side of the pool are their parents—just in case you wondered. Of late I've made a strong point that their parents must be present. I'm sure you understand.'

Betsy Clendenin had alleged in her book that Jonathan had paid parents large amounts of money to let—in fact, to teach and to

69

require—their prepubertal daughters to entertain him with oral sex, two or three of them at a time. She had written also that he paid attractive young prostitutes lavish fees to submit to sadism: whippings and other torments. He was incapable, she had said, of engaging in normal sex, so got what satisfaction he could from a sex-fantasy world he could afford to create.

'None of my business,' said Columbo dryly.

'Your business is the death of Betsy Clendenin. I saw on television that you are investigating the explosion. I suppose I'm a suspect.'

'Until we find out who did it, everybody's a suspect,' said Columbo. Then he lifted his eyebrows and turned up the palms of his hands. 'Of course, some people are more likely suspects than others.'

'Like me.'

'Yes, Sir, like you. You gotta admit, you had motive.'

'The woman did a character assassination on me unparalleled in the history of yellow journalism.'

'I haven't read it.'

'God bless you, Lieutenant Columbo.'

'I guess Mrs. Columbo read a part of it in some magazine.'

'*Glitz*. You put that disreputable woman away on ice. Ai-ling Cooper-Svan, I mean. I knew Gunnar. He was not a nice man. But she—' Jonathan shook his head.

'Bashed his head in,' Columbo finished the thought.

'Didn't she just. Anyway, you imagine I had a motive to kill Betsy Clendenin. I agree I did, a better motive than most of the many people who had a motive. But I didn't do it, Lieutenant. What is more, I didn't hire the someone who did.'

'Where were you Thursday night, if ya don't mind my asking?

'Right here, where I always am when I'm not out performing. Lieutenant . . . *have mercy!* You're looking at a man who can't see well enough to drive a car. You're looking at a man who has some difficulty controlling his body. You're looking at a man who can't have ordinary friendships with ordinary people because he's a freak. And you're looking at a man who found a way to cope with some of this, only to have some spiteful bitch attack him and try to destroy him—for money, for profit, for no better motive. I'm not sorry she's dead. I'm sorry she died so quickly, with so little suffering. But I didn't kill her, and I didn't employ someone to kill her for me.'

The houseman put Columbo's Scotch on the table beside him.

'You could have done it, and you'd have liked to do it—but you didn't. Okay. I've got no evidence that says you did.'

Jonathan may have been staring intently at

71

Columbo. With his eyes hidden behind his sunglasses, it was impossible to tell. Columbo studied him for a moment, realized he couldn't read the man's expression, and picked up his Scotch.

'I'm sure you know the meaning of the word pyrotechnics,' said Jonathan.

'Yes, Sir.'

'Take a look at Miss Clendenin's book about me. On page 151 she accuses me of having had a homosexual relationship with a man named Weldon James. Poor Weldon. He *is* gay, of course, but he'd stayed in the closet until *she* made fun of him. We didn't have any relationship whatever, I swear to you. But the man who did was so embarrassed that he abandoned Weldon and left him alone and devastated. Weldon is one of the film industry's finest pyrotechnicians. If anyone knows how to set off an explosion, he does. I regard him as a friend and am certain he didn't do it, but you'll find out about him sooner or later, and it would be well if his name were cleared sooner rather than later.'

'I see. I thank ya. I'll make a point of checking out Mr. James.'

'Acquaint yourself with her publishing history, Lieutenant. She was a destructive woman, who went about wreaking havoc on people whose success she envied.'

Columbo swallowed Scotch. 'I really do have to get back to town, Sir. I thank ya for the drink and for the look at a wonderful estate.'

'Come back any time,' said Jonathan. 'Come when you can spend more time. Come when you can take an hour or so to swim.'

'Would ya believe it? I *can't* swim,' Columbo said as he rose and looked toward the house.

Jonathan grinned. 'My nymphs will teach you.'

'Uh . . . yeah. Well, I'm not sure I—'

'Any time, Lieutenant. You will always be welcome.'

'Thank ya. I thank ya. Oh, say, there was one little thing I wanted to ask. Your security men. They're from—?'

'Detwiler Services, Lieutenant. They've done this work for me for years.'

'Detwiler . . . Right. I've heard of them. Never had any complaint, huh?'

Jonathan shook his head. 'Efficient, loyal. . . everything I could ask for.'

'Well, thank ya again. You have a nice afternoon, Sir.'

14

MONDAY, JANUARY 4—2:30 P.M.

Fritz sat beside Meredith Nelson in the small Catholic church. A memorial service for Betsy Clendenin was underway. There was no casket. The county medical examiner had not yet released the body; and probably, in any

73

event, not many wanted to stare at a casket that could contain nothing but bits and pieces.

He held Meredith's hand. A few people had already noticed and were smiling at the blossoming friendship between the man in his seventies, known more in this town as a successful and wealthy real-estate agent than as a retired FBI agent, and the flashy late-middle-aged actress who even on this occasion was dressed as she invariably was in her soap-opera role: in a dress that was short and tight, this one of course black.

Fritz had no interest in what they thought. Meredith pleased him. The only thing she had done that did not please him was tearfully ask him to come with her and hold her hand during the service for her dear friend.

So here he was. He looked around him and wondered who all these people were who had come to a solemn memorial service for the whore. He wondered if any of them were her victims, come to laugh inside when she was eulogized.

He took special notice of a spectacular redhead—and didn't know she was Adrienne Boswell. Neither did he recognize Bill Lloyd, acting editor of *Glitz* during the imprisonment of Ai-ling Cooper. He didn't recognize Bruce Emerson, manager and business partner of the rock-and-rap singer Jonathan. He didn't recognize the man sitting beside Emerson—Marcus Detwiler, president of the security company that guarded the singer and owner of a substantial interest in Jonathan Enterprises, Incorporated. He had never heard the name of the third man in the trio: Seizo Asano, president of Asano Electronics, the company that produced all of Jonathan's records and tapes.

The eulogy was spoken by Walter Mahaffey, the whore's publisher, who had the effrontery to describe her as 'a woman of boundless energy, a major talent, and a journalist of flawless integrity.'

A sudden jarring thought came to Fritz Kloss. Was it possible the whore had supplied copies of her work to Mahaffey? If she had, blowing her away had been for nothing. He couldn't do the same to Mahaffey.

What a thought!

He drove Meredith home. 'It was a touching service,' she said. 'Betsy deserved every word spoken of her, and more. I can't believe she's dead. I can't believe anyone would want to kill her.'

'She made a lot of enemies, I guess,' said Fritz.

'Oh, but to *kill* her!'

'You think she's some kind of martyr?'

Meredith nodded. 'Absolutely. Did you notice who was there? The three men who own and control Jonathan. She cost them a billion dollars. More.'

'Freak,' Fritz muttered scornfully.

'A whole friggin' industry, Fritz! Don't you understand? She destroyed it.'

'How? What'd she do to him, exactly?'

'Don't you know? Well . . . you come in and sit down in the living room, and I'll hand you her book. Then you can figure it out.'

5:00 P.M.

She poured him a Beefeater, and he took off his shoes and sat down in a recliner with *The Real Jonathan* by Betsy Clendenin.

Some of it was pretty strong stuff—

His publicity staff has insisted on the point that Kitty Lockhart's mother was present whenever Kitty was with Jonathan. She was; that's true. What the Jonathan, Incorporated public-relations department omits to tell is that the mother is a pitiful crack addict with a very expensive habit. So completely enslaved to crack is Kitty's mother that she eagerly sold her daughter to sustain her habit. What is more, once she had smoked her ration of crack, she would be too dreamy and addled to have any idea what Jonathan and Kitty were doing.

What Jonathan and Kitty were doing beggars description. It can be described in Kitty's innocent four-letter words, or it can be described in clinical terms. Either way it is nauseating, sickening conduct on the part of a thirty-two-year-old pervert against a twelve-year-old child.

This much of Kitty's statement we can quote—"Mommy had told me what Jonathan would want me to do. I didn't think it was the right thing to do, but Mommy said it was, and after all, he *was* Jonathan. But I gotta say, the first time, I threw up. I couldn't help it; I just threw up. Jonathan laughed. Then—Well, I guess I laughed, too. The next time I didn't throw up.

'Penny did once, when it was *her third time*. We all got a big ha-ha out of that, even Penny. I don't know what was the matter with Penny that time. I mean, you get used to it pretty quick, y'know. Y'know?'

Fritz put down the book. 'Do you believe this?' he asked Meredith.

'They didn't sue her for libel.'

'But—How come this guy's not in the slammer for corrupting the morals of—'

'Read on,' said Meredith.

A month after Kitty Lockhart spoke into this writer's tape recorder, she disappeared, as did her mother, Bea. It required two months of investigation to learn what happened to the mother and daughter. They are alive and well. They live in the Brazilian city of Manaus, on the Upper Amazon. Kitty has a three-bedroom apartment of her own, in a modern high-rise building. Technically, the apartment is her mother's, but Bea actually lives in a detox clinic just outside the city, where she will remain for a year. Kitty does not go to school. She has not learned a word of Portuguese. She has a boyfriend, the son of another expatriate American. She is fourteen years old and pregnant.

Brazil would not force Kitty to return to the States, even if our government asked for her. She is a witness, not charged with any crime. If she were charged with anything, it could only be juvenile delinquency. As for the mother, well, Brazil does not like to extradite. Anyway, the only witness against her is Kitty herself, who is not about to testify.

Another nymph who served Jonathan may not have fared so well. The Penny mentioned by Kitty is nowhere to be found, nor is her father who apparently was the one who sold Penny to Jonathan. Her real name is Penelope Kent, and the father is Edward Kent. Both of them have disappeared. They may be in Brazil, too; but if they are, this writer has not been able to locate them.

Fritz put down the book. 'Don't you think Miss Clendenin made up a lot of what she wrote?'

'If she wasn't telling the truth in that book,

why didn't Jonathan's handlers sue for libel? I told you, she destroyed a billion-dollar industry. He's not much in demand anymore—not like he used to be, anyway.'

'Do you suppose they killed her?' Fritz asked.

15

Columbo sat down with Adrienne at a table in Fonda la Paloma. She was still wearing the black dress she had worn to Betsy Clendenin's memorial service.

'This was her favorite watering hole,' said Adrienne. 'It may tell you something about her.'

'In my experience you really don't find out much about people by visiting their favorite bars,' said Columbo. Adrienne grinned. 'I'm an evil woman, Columbo. I wanted to have a drink with you. I want you to use your influence and do something for me.'

'What kinda influence do I have that could do anything for you?'

'I want to be put on the authorized visitors list for Ai-ling Cooper. I want to talk to her. Betsy Clendenin visited her two weeks before she was murdered. Betsy didn't go up there just because the two of them were old buddies. She had a reason. She was working on something. Ai-ling may know what. Remember what you said—that blowing Betsy away was a pretty drastic way to take revenge on her; more likely it was to prevent her publishing something new.'

Columbo nodded. 'I'll see to it you get in to see her. On a condition. I want to know what she tells you.'

'I never thought of it any other way.'

'There's a curious little fact about the Clendenin murder that bothers me,' said Columbo. 'You know how things get stuck on your mind and you can't forget 'em? Well, this one is stuck on me, and I can't forget it. It probably doesn't mean anything at all, but—'

'What is it, man? Spit it out.'

'Well . . . when the explosion went off and killed Miss Clendenin, she was stark, staring naked. Why would that be? She was alone. She had to be alone. Nobody else was killed in the house. So why was she naked?'

Adrienne grinned. 'The image preys on your mind, huh?'

'It's an odd fact, an unusual fact. In my experience, when a fact is entirely inconsistent with all the other facts, it means somethin'. She was killed in her office, not in her bedroom or her bathroom. So why was she—'

'Columbo. Betsy was what you might call full-figured and probably wore a lot of spandex she was glad to be out of. I don't think your little fact is mysterious.'

'Okay. Guess where I've been.'

'Where?'

'Xanadu.'

Adrienne smiled. ' "In Xanadu did Kubla Khan a stately pleasure-dome decree." '

'Ya got me there. How's that go?'

Adrienne recited—

'"In Xanadu did Kubla Khan
A stately pleasure-dome decree:
Where Alph, the sacred river, ran
Through caverns measureless to man
Down to a sunless sea.
So twice five miles of fertile ground
With walls and towers were girdled round:
And there were gardens bright with sinuous
	rills,
Where blossomed many an incense-bearing
	tree;
And here were forests ancient as the hills,
Enfolding sunny spots of greenery." '

'Yeah,' Columbo said. 'Yeah. That's the place. I don't understand every word of that, but that describes it. Who wrote that?'

'Samuel Taylor Coleridge.'

'Well, now, Mrs. Columbo might know about that. She takes night classes at the university. Coleridge . . . Coleridge. I'll remember that and mention it to her.'

'How were you received at Xanadu?'

'Well—Once I got past the goons that guard the place, I was treated like a prince.'

Adrienne sighed. 'Those 'goons' are capable

81

of killing even an LAPD detective and dumping his body. I have to figure they didn't think you had anything strong against Jonathan.'

Columbo shrugged. 'I don't.'

'He impressed you as—'

'Not able to do anything bad, much.'

'He's not able, not any. He was a billion-dollar property, as a freak. Columbo, *millions* of people worshiped him as a god. Hundreds of thousands still do. He was the biggest thing since the greaseball junkie.'

'Greaseball . . . ?'

'*Ell*-viss. If Betsy had done a thing on Presley like she did on Jonathan—'

I get your point. But it's done. Killing her doesn't bring it back. If anything, it gets it *more* publicity. I—'

'Detwiler doesn't forgive easy,' said Adrienne.

'Detwiler?'

'Marcus Detwiler is president of Detwiler Security Services. The goons you referred to are Detwiler's goons. But Detwiler doesn't just guard Jonathan. He owns a piece of him. He was at the memorial service for Betsy. So was Bruce Emerson, Jonathan's manager, who also owns a piece. So was Seizo Asano, who doesn't own a piece but was making ten fortunes out of Jonathan's exclusive recording contract with Asano Electronics.'

'Why were they at her memorial service?'

'Who knows? To be sure she was dead, maybe. To gloat. She cost them a lot of money.'

Columbo shook his head. 'Seems to have cost several people a lot of money.'

'Columbo, if you're investigating the murder of Betsy Clendenin, you've got to read some of her stuff. Stop by my place, and I'll lend you two or three of her books.'

7:21 P.M.

Ai-ling Cooper sat at the small table in her cell, writing a letter. She was allowed to have a portable self-correcting typewriter, a sort of primitive word processor, and she turned out a great deal of copy in the course of a week. Tonight she was writing a letter to Bill Lloyd, who was acting editor-in-chief of *Glitz* during her imprisonment.

```
You have the Clendenin piece that I
sent you just after she visited me
here in December. Her death puts a
new value on that, so let's give it
a more prominent place and beef it
up with a story about her murder.
   What is far more important is
that    she    told    me    she    had
information   to   the   effect   that
Hoover    lifted    confidential    FBI
files  and  turned  them  over  to  Roy
```

83

Cohn, not when he was with McCarthy
but when he was a lawyer in New
York. Now, I suppose, there's not
going to be any book.

Which is the point. You should
get in touch with Walter Mahaffey
and find out if she had given him
any chapters. I doubt if she had
written this chapter, because she
was still researching it. But she
might have shown Mahaffey
something. Also please call Dave
Peavy, her agent, and see what he
knows. If there isn't going to be a
book, there might be some damned
hot stuff that we can run.

She pulled a pack of Marlboros from the
pocket of her terry-cloth robe and used a
paper match—they weren't allowed to have
lighters—to light it. She reread the letter,
trying to decide if there were anything more
she should tell Bill at the moment.

'Hey, Eileen.' Most of the women in the
prison thought her name was Eileen. 'Could
you lend a gal a smoke?'

'Sure.' She shook another cigarette from her
pack, got up, and passed it out between the
cell bars, to the woman's hand that was thrust
over to receive it. 'Need a match?'

I got a match. Thanks.'

'Okay, Sally.'

Oddly—or maybe not so oddly—Sally really would pay her back. The girl was twenty-one years old and had been here two years. She was doing twenty-five years to life for killing a rival crack dealer. She was a wisp of a girl, and it was difficult to think of her murdering someone. Ai-ling had briefly thought about writing a piece on her, then decided publicity could not do Sally any good.

```
Betsy told me she was going to
interview a retired FBI agent who
might know something about the Roy
Cohn business. I've racked my brain
trying to think of the name.
```

16

TUESDAY, JANUARY 5—10:11 A.M.

Captain Sczciegel (who pronounced his name 'Seagul') greeted Columbo in a corridor at Parker Center. 'I'll be damned if I don't see your sidearm hanging under your arm,' he said. 'Good work, Columbo!'

'Well, I . . . uh . . . *promised* ya I'd be better about that and do the regulation thing as much as I could, after you got me that dispensation and let me carry this trusty old gun and not have to carry that Beretta.'

'I'm afraid to ask if it's loaded,' said the Captain, only half facetiously. 'You *do* have rounds in the chamber, don't you. Please tell me you do.'

'Well, I don't figure there's any reason to carry it loaded here in the office. Accidents can happen, y'know. I got bullets in my car.'

'And you'll load it when you get in the car? You'll put rounds in—?'

'Oh, sure.' Columbo nodded. Since the captain didn't ask, he didn't tell him he'd also shove the revolver under the seat as soon as he left headquarters. Together with the holster. He felt foolish wearing a holster with no gun in it.

'Well, what about the Clendenin case?' asked Captain Sczciegel.

'See how red my eyes are, Captain? I was up half the night reading some of her books.'

'Learn anything?'

'Only that half the people in Los Angeles and a lot of people other places might have wanted to kill her. What do we know about a man named Marcus Detwiler?'

'It's a well-known name. Check with Bunko.'

When Columbo sat down at his desk, he found a note from Martha Zimmer—

Federal Express has checked its records and finds that it did not deliver a package to Betsy Clendenin at any time during the two weeks preceding the explosion.

10:34 A.M.

'Hiya, Murph! Anybody got any good scams goin' these days?'

'Hey, Columbo. Scams? How could you ask? We live in L.A., don't we? *Everybody's* a hustler.'

'Shoulda tried living in N' Yawk, where I grew up, ya wanta see hustlers.'

'Hollywood,' said Murphy. 'The biggest scams in the world.'

'Well . . . let's not have a braggin' contest about it.'

'What can I do for you, Columbo? Want a cuppa?'

'Sure.'

They walked to the coffee room and returned to Murphy's desk.

Detective Sergeant Pat Murphy was a florid Irishman with a nose like W. C. Fields's—and for the same reason. He never drank on duty or came to duty after drinking, but he was sober very few hours of his off-days. Divorced and living alone, he liked to do his drinking in a pub, socializing with the men who drank there. A new joke never came into circulation that he didn't hear and remember.

'Hey, Columbo, you hear the one about the guy who went to the doctor and said he wanted

87

a vasectomy? The doc asked him if he'd talked the idea over with his wife and kids. He said, 'Yeah, and they took a vote. The idea won, twelve to three.' What can I do for you, Columbo?'

'What you got, if anything, on a guy named Marcus Detwiler?'

'Nothing. I know who you mean. We got nothing on him. That company of his, though, is something else. He seems to make a point of hiring guys with criminal records. There've been a lot of complaints, some arrests, a few convictions.'

'For what?'

'Detwiler Security Services hires out guards for estates and businesses. Those guards have a way of beating up on people. One of them shot a man two or three years ago. Too many incidents like that. Off the record, Columbo, just between you and me there's gotta be something screwy about anybody who'd hire Detwiler Security Services. It makes me suspicious every time I hear about it. There are plenty of respectable security services around town, but Detwiler ain't one of them.'

'Captain Semiegel suggested Bunko would know something about Detwiler. What would that be, Murph?'

Murphy took a swallow of coffee. 'Does Homicide get any better coffee than this?' He shook his head. 'Why does LAPD have the worst coffee in town, 'specially when guys on the job have to drink so damn much of it? Still off the record. There's reason to think that Detwiler takes on clients who want to hide something, then blackmails them. Can't prove it, but there it is; that's probably what Sczciegel was talking about. Like I said, there's got to be something wrong when somebody hires Detwiler for security.'

'Could somebody hire 'em to do a hit, ya figure?' Columbo asked.

'Like blow away Betsy Clendenin? That what ya got in mind?'

Columbo nodded. 'That's what I got in mind. Like blow away Betsy Clendenin.'

Murphy shrugged. 'Your problem, Columbo. I wouldn't know.'

1:49 P.M.

'Columbo. Lieutenant Columbo, LAPD Homicide. I've got a two o'clock appointment with Mr. Peavy. I'm a little early. Usually am. I've got a way of showin' up places before I'm suppose to be there.'

The secretary he was talking to was an exceptionally handsome young black woman. 'I do have you on his appointment book for two o'clock, Lieutenant. He's with a client. I'm sure he'll be ready to see you at two.'

'I'll wait,' said Columbo.

'I'm sorry.'

'Not at all. I'm early. Anyway, waiting is a

89

big part of what I do for a living. Uh . . . you wouldn't happen to have a little salt in your desk, would ya? You know, like a little envelope like ya get at McDonald's or some place?'

She smiled, showing flawless white teeth. 'Well—' From a drawer she produced a little envelope of salt.

'I thank ya. I do thank ya,' said Columbo. He sat down, pulled a hard-boiled egg from his raincoat pocket, rolled the egg between his hands to crack the shell, peeled off the shell, sprinkled on a little salt, and began contentedly to munch on the egg. 'Didn't have time for lunch today,' he explained. 'It's the perfect thing, ya know, for nourishment and tasting good. Mrs. Columbo keeps a bowl of 'em in the fridge, and I take a couple with me every day. One day I took a couple that hadn't been boiled. What a mess!'

He had just finished his egg and was depositing the shell in the secretary's trash basket when David Peavy opened his office door and asked the secretary to pull the Dunedin file. He looked with amused curiosity at the disheveled man in the wrinkled, stained raincoat.

'Ah! You're Lieutenant . . . Columbo?'

'Right. I'm early. I was telling Miss—Well, your secretary here that I gotta awful habit of getting places early. It's not the best habit in the world, but I just don't seem to be able to

90

break it.'

'Come on in. Come right in. I'm auditioning a little girl. Let's see what you think of her.'

Columbo went into the inner office. It was a big room, facing broad windows. Three walls were covered with autographed pictures of the performers and writers represented by the Peavy Agency.

'Cathy, this is Lieutenant Columbo of the Los Angeles police. He's a homicide detective.'

Cathy was eighteen or nineteen years old. Her wraparound skirt and a little jacket lay on the couch. She wore a black leotard and ballet slippers. Her legs were bare.

'Do a little of the 'understand' number for the Lieutenant,' said Peavy. 'Here. I'll start the disk.'

Columbo recognized the music. It was from the soundtrack for *Gigi*. The girl sang, 'I don't understand the Parisians. . .' and accompanied the song with a balletic dance. When she finished, he nodded and grinned and clapped his hands.

'Take a seat outside and wait a little while, Cathy,' said Peavy. I have to talk with the Lieutenant.' When the girl closed the door behind her, he shook his head and told Columbo, 'I'm afraid I can't do a thing for her. I mean, she's got talent, Lieutenant. But where am I going to place her? The shit that's run on the boob tube today, there's no place for talent

91

like that. The kid's mother encouraged her to learn to sing and dance, and what good's it ever going to do her? A damned shame.'

Columbo frowned and shook his head.

'Lieutenant, if I had a young Judy Garland for a client, I couldn't get a gig for her. Ho! If she wanted to work topless or nude—But Cathy doesn't want to do that.'

'Shame,' said Columbo.

'I see you smoke cigars,' said Peavy. 'Try one of mine.' He opened a humidor on his desk and took out a cigar for Columbo and one for himself. Peavy was a man in his forties, as Columbo judged, a somewhat stocky man with a full head of wavy light-brown hair, blue eyes, a strong cleft chin, handsomely dressed in a sand-colored cashmere jacket over a dark-green golf shirt. 'Well,' he said when he had his cigar lighted. 'I suppose you want to talk about Betsy Clendenin.'

'Yes, Sir. Uh . . . can I borrow your lighter?'

'Oh. Certainly. Sorry. Betsy's death is a damned tragedy, Lieutenant Columbo. The woman was a crusader.'

'Did she make a lot of money?' Columbo asked.

'A very great deal of money, yes. Her books were bestsellers, invariably. She sold magazine articles. She did lecture tours. She was a dynamo of energy.'

'I went through three of her books last night. I can see why somebody might want to kill her. I got no choice; I have to look at every one of the people who might hate her so much they'd want to kill her. But I got a different idea about the case. I don't think she was necessarily killed for revenge. Somebody went to a whole lotta trouble, blowing up a whole house. I have to wonder if somebody wasn't trying to stop her from publishing something and blew up her house to destroy her notes and manuscript. I understand she was working on a book about J. Edgar Hoover, which was gonna tell some bad things. What I'm hoping is that she turned over some of that book to you, so we can know who all was going to be mentioned.'

Peavy shook his head. 'I'm afraid not. It is true that an author proposing a book normally submits a detailed outline, but Betsy was so successful that she was able to skip that step. She and I simply sat down over lunch with Walter Mahaffey, and she told him what she wanted to do. He bought the book on the basis of her statement.'

'She must have told something about what she planned to expose,' said Columbo.

'Well . . . I remember being disappointed at first. She was going to write about Hoover's being a homosexual, which is old stuff, well known; it's been done. Then she said something about a relationship between Hoover and Roy Cohn.'

'Roy Cohn didn't kill her, for sure,' said

Columbo. 'He's dead,'

'No. He sure didn't. Died of AIDS, years ago.'

'You suppose she gave her publisher some advance work to look at?'

Peavy shook his head. 'I'd be surprised if she did. Betsy didn't work that way. But—I can call Walter Mahaffey and ask him.'

'I'd appreciate that.'

Peavy buzzed his secretary and told her to get Mahaffey on the phone.

'This is a fine cigar, Mr. Peavy.'

Peavy opened the box. 'Have a couple more,' he said. 'I hope you catch the killer, Lieutenant. I really do. Apart from losing a talented client and a dear personal friend, I'll be losing some big commissions.'

'She seems to have cost some other people some very big money,' said Columbo. 'I went out to talk to Jonathan yesterday. I keep coming across the name Detwiler.'

'I couldn't testify that Detwiler threatened us when the Jonathan book was being written, but somebody did. Somebody threatened Betsy and me—and even Walter Mahaffey, who's in New York.'

'Phone calls?'

'Yes.

'Did you call the police?'

'And say what? That we'd had anonymous phone calls? Were we supposed to ask LAPD to put permanent guards on our homes and

94

offices? I notified building security here. I beefed up my home alarm system. And I bought another pistol.'

Columbo puffed on his cigar and said nothing.

'Could have been crank calls,' said Peavy. 'Betsy would go on television and talk about the book she was writing. She'd whet the public appetite for it. So people knew she was going to do a job on Jonathan, months before her book came out. He had fans who would have killed to protect him—and probably still does. To a few young people, Jonathan can do no wrong. Even now, even with what we know about him. There are young people who don't care about anything like that. Makes you think about the loss of values and all that.'

'But he did lose most of his fans.'

'Right. He came out of it reasonably well. The story is around that Xanadu is for sale, that he doesn't make enough money to maintain it. But he'll live very comfortably for the rest of his life. Can't say as much for Barbara Henry or for Senator Scott. Betsy really ruined them.'

'I read some of what she said about them. If what she said was true, maybe they deserved to be ruined.'

'It was true. But they're bitter—very, very bitter. Scott thought he was going to run for President of the United States. He might have, and he might have won, too. He called Betsy and threatened her. He said he'd sue her, and she said go ahead; then he said maybe there were other ways of getting at her. And Barbara Henry stalked her for a while. Anyway, Betsy thought she did.'

'I guess I'll have to talk to them.'

'Be prepared to meet two people who'll tell you they're glad Betsy is dead.'

The telephone buzzed. Peavy picked it up. 'Okay,' he said. 'Thanks.' He shrugged. 'Walter Mahaffey isn't in right now. Shall I set up an appointment for you?'

'If you don't mind.'

Peavy spoke with the publisher's secretary in New York, then turned to Columbo and said, 'She says he'll be in his office at six o'clock, New York time. You want to call him then?'

'Yes. I'll call him at six, New York time.'

'Well, then—If there's anything else I can do for you, let me know.'

PART THREE

'There's no limit to dumb,' Barbara Henry said bitterly.

'You're tellin'me?' Columbo shrugged.

'It's common knowledge that coons have bigger whangs than white men—which makes them more lubricious. That's what makes them so dangerous to white women.'

—JOHN EDGAR HOOVER

Six o'clock New York time was three o'clock L.A. time, and Columbo sat at his desk, ready to make the call. He had not taken off his raincoat. The stub of Peavy's fine cigar was in one pocket, and he pulled it out and put it in his mouth. If he lit it, some people would frown and stare at him. People hadn't used to do that, but they did it now.

Peavy's secretary had written down for him the telephone number of Walter Mahaffey in New York. He waited a couple of minutes, to give the man a little time, then punched in the New York number.

He got one of those automated telephone-answering services. 'If you are calling from a touch-tone phone, enter '1' *now*.'—'If you know the extension number of the party with whom you wish to speak, enter that number now. If you know the name of your party, enter the first five letters of that person's last name, using the keypad on your touch-tone telephone.'

Lord! Okay, M was 6, A was 2 . . . and so on. 6 2 4 2 3.

'Mr. Mahaffey's office.'

'Ma'am, I'm glad to be speaking with a real human being at last. This is Lieutenant Columbo in Los Angeles. I believe Mr.

Mahaffey is expecting me.'

'Yes, Sir. I'll put him on the line.'

Well—He wondered how many times today she had been told someone was glad to be speaking with a real human being at last. So many times she'd lost all sense of humor about it, no doubt.

'Lieutenant Columbo! This is Walter Mahaffey.'

The voice was big and jovial. Columbo wondered what Mahaffey looked like.

'Sir, I guess Mr. Peavy's secretary told your secretary that I'm investigating the death of Miss Clendenin. I was kind of hoping you might have some information that would help me.'

'Anything I've got is yours, Lieutenant. I'm afraid I don't have anything, though. I flew out for her memorial service yesterday, and if I'd been aware of any way I could help, I'd have called you.'

'Yes, Sir. I appreciate that. Sometimes, though, people have information they don't realize will be important to an investigation.'

'As I said, anything I've got is yours. Any questions I can answer, I'll answer.'

'Alright, Sir. One thing I'm wonderin' is, how close was she to being finished with her Hoover book?'

'I'd guess it was three-quarters finished. But that is a guess. I don't really know.'

'Had she sent along part of it?'

'Yes, she had. I've got about two hundred pages. She sent it on a computer disk, and we printed it here.'

'The way I understand it,' said Columbo, 'she pretty well took Mr. Hoover apart. And Mr. Tolson. But they're both dead, so obviously they had nothing to do with the murder. My question is, what's in the manuscript, if anything, that some *living* person wouldn't want to come out—wouldn't want it so bad that he'd *kill* Miss Clendenin to stop her from publishing it.'

'That's a little difficult to say. After all, J. Edgar Hoover's been dead almost thirty years. But there are still those who worship at his shrine. We've had calls and letters telling us that we're Communists or liberals or whatever. There are some Hoover fanatics out there, Lieutenant. Still.'

'But is there anyone who could be hurt by what she was going to tell? You have any idea?'

'Let me send you a copy of what she sent me. I'll FedEx it to you in the morning.'

'I'll appreciate it.'

'I hope to god you catch the murderer. I'm not going to feel entirely safe until you do.'

'I'm doin' my best, Sir. Just pickin' up little bits and pieces of information from here and there, trying to fit them together in some way that makes sense.'

'As I said, anything I can do—'

'Uh, well maybe there is one more little thing. She doesn't seem to have had a secretary. She doesn't seem to have had anybody that worked with her. Would you know about that? I mean, she was an awful productive woman. Did she have anybody that helped her?'

'Well, sure, Lieutenant. Hasn't anybody mentioned Linda Semon?'

'No. Nobody has.'

'Linda did research work for Betsy. You should talk to her.'

*   *   *

Columbo went home for dinner, then went out again, to visit the nightclub where Barbara Henry worked. He was surprised that anyone would call a nightclub Casa Rameras, The Whorehouse. Very few Angelenos didn't know what it meant. The Vice Squad knew what it meant, and when he walked into the place the first person he saw was Duke Palma, a veteran vice detective.

'Columbo! Somebody kill somebody?'

'Naa, Duke. Naw. Maybe a witness here. I don't know.'

Duke Palma was as old as Columbo, but he was a fitness freak and was straight and slender and muscular. In years past he had urged Columbo to join him at his gym, where he would help Columbo become a new man.

102

'Who's your witness?'

'Barbara Henry.'

Duke Palma nodded toward the bar. 'That's your girl.'

Columbo recognized her. He had seen her on television many times, on a comedy show Mrs. Columbo favored. She had played an innocent opposite two dissolute and sharp-tongued roommates sharing a New York apartment. Here, she was one of three topless barmaids working behind the bar: by far the most attractive of the three.

'Y'know the story?' Duke asked.

Columbo knew the story. Her real name was Henrietta Barbieri. She had struggled for years to get a part in something: a movie, best of all, a television show, a dinner theater . . . anything. She developed a shtick: to drop her jaw and widen her eyes when a wisecracking actor or—better—actress spoke a double entendre, pretending she didn't quite understand the line and yet suspected it meant more than it said. In her first season on television she was strictly a supporting player, a third banana, appearing on only a few of the shows. In her second season she was second banana and appeared on all the shows. In her third season she was the star. Between that season and the next, she made a comedy film.

Then—An article by Betsy Clendenin. Henrietta Barbieri was a rarity, a recovered crackhead. From age eighteen to twenty she had been a down-the-drain addict who had done whatever she had to do to support the habit. Driven by the implacable demand, she had committed muggings, she had become a shoplifter, she had stolen a car. Repeatedly, she had sold herself into prostitution to get the money she needed to cop a few cracks. She became pregnant. The baby was born addicted. It died. By the time the doctors figured out what had killed the baby, the young mother had disappeared. This was in Florida. She mugged a drunken tourist to buy what she had to have and fled to Atlantic City. There she became pregnant again. Terrified lest this baby die too and she be charged with something terrible, she tried to break the habit. She couldn't. She bore the second child in a hospital in Connecticut. The baby survived, but it was mentally defective. Henrietta Barbieri was arrested and committed to the Connecticut Women's Prison at Niantic. There she climbed the walls; but, compelled to go cold turkey, suffering the agonies of hell, and with the help of a sympathetic medical staff, she broke the addiction. After seventeen months she was released and eventually made her way to California and stardom.

Much of this her fans might have forgiven. That she had not tried to find the defective child and at least offer support for it, they could not. But for that, wrote Betsy Clendenin, she might have let it stand and not exposed the secrets of Barbara Henry. *That* she could not overlook. *That* the television audience would not overlook. Barbara Henry's career ended.

'Phil.' With a gesture, Duke Palma summoned a man. 'This,' he said to Columbo, 'is the crumb-bum that runs this joint.'

'What's up, Duke?' asked a sharp-nosed man with great black eyebrows and slicked-down black hair. 'This is Lieutenant Columbo, Homicide. He wants to talk to Bobby.'

'Is that broad in trouble? Is she makin' trouble?'

'Nothin' like that,' said Columbo. 'Just might have a little information I can use.'

'Ya wanta take her in?'

'Nothin' like that. Just wanta ask her a few questions. Take five minutes.'

'At the bar okay? Guys like to look at her.'

'Okay.'

Phil led Columbo to the bar, curtly gestured to Barbara Henry that she should come to the end, where a few stools were empty. 'I'll keep stiffs away from ya,' he said, taking a stool a short distance down the bar. 'Bobby, this is Lieutenant Columbo, a homicide detective. He wants to talk to ya. Give him whatever he wants, on the house.'

She was an exceptionally handsome woman, showing almost no sign of the ravaging lifetime she had lived. A thin white scar in her left eyebrow was the only suggestion that she had

105

known difficult times. Otherwise, her features were regular and attractive. She had glossy dark-brown hair, which she wore long, to her shoulders, brushed down smooth. A small gold cross hung on a delicate chain around her neck. Her bare breasts were small and firm. She wore black bikini panties and net stockings held up by crimson garters.

'What would you like to drink?' she asked dully.

'Scotch,' he said. 'With a little soda.'

She took a bottle of Chivas from the shelf and poured him what had to be a triple. 'New Year's Eve I was here all evening,' she said. 'I got two dozen witnesses. More.'

'Figures,' said Columbo.

'Do you want me to tell you I'm sorry she's dead? Forget it. I'm *glad* she's dead. I'm only sorry she could only die once.'

'I don't figure you killed her. What's more, I doubt you could afford what somebody may have been paid to kill her. But you might know somethin' I don't know, that I ought to know.'

'You know something, Lieutenant? I don't suppose one guy in twenty who sits here at the bar and talks with me has any idea what Betsy Clendenin did to me. Even guys who recognize me as the airhead from TV don't know why I'm not on TV anymore. They *ask me*. They ask me, for Christ sake! There's no limit to dumb,' Barbara Henry said bitterly.

106

'You're tellin'me?' Columbo shrugged.

'Why'd she have to do it to me? Why couldn't she have left me alone? I'll tell you why. For *money*. She claimed she didn't like the way I abandoned my baby. What she ignored was that the baby was *adopted* and was living—is *still* living with folks that love her. She didn't need to know her mommy's not her *real* mommy. Miss Holier-than-thou Clendenin didn't ask *why* I didn't try to get in touch with my daughter. She just made a judgment and set out to ruin my life—that is, to ruin the life I'd finally made after living my own little hell for three years. Where was her goddamned charity, Lieutenant?'

'You're not the only person who thinks that way,' said Columbo. He took a sip of Scotch.

'I've read her obits. What a *heroine* she was! What a goody-two-shoes!'

'Did she interview you?'

'Hell, no! She didn't want to hear *my* side. Journalistic ethics. An oxymoron, Lieutenant Columbo. There's no such thing.'

'Why ya workin' here, if you don't mind my askin'?'

'I make more money here than I'd make as a waitress or a dime-store clerk. That and this is about all I know how to do—that and turning tricks, which I'm *never* going to do again. Anyway, I've got no pride left. She took that away from me.'

'So you hated her. What did ya do about it?'

Barbara Henry shrugged. 'What *could* I do?'

'Probably nothin'.' He took another drink of scotch. 'So you didn't do anything? It just sort of . . . burns inside ya.'

'Something like that.'

'Well, I thank ya. Thank you for your time. I, uh, feel like I oughta leave you a tip, since you'd have been makin' some if you hadn't been standing here talking to me.'

'Forget it. I got a *little* dignity left.'

'Okay.' He slipped off the bar stool and stepped one pace away. Then he turned. 'Oh, say, there is one little thing I guess I should mention. Probably doesn't amount to anything. But—Miss Clendenin told somebody you followed her around for a while. Stalked her. Anything to that?'

Barbara Henry glanced around her. 'Is that a crime?' she asked quietly.

'Maybe. Maybe not.'

'I wanted to see if I could find something on her, that *I* could publish.' She shrugged again. 'Another dumb idea. Who'd believe me, against Miss Goody-two-shoes?'

'Didn't find out anything anyway,' Colombo suggested.

'Not exactly.'

'Something?'

'She had two lovers. One of them might have been jealous of the other.'

'Can you identify them?'

'No.'

'Then how do you know they were her lovers?' Colombo asked.

'Casual friends don't usually stay at people's homes all night,' said Barbara Henry. 'And get a passionate kiss in the doorway at six in the morning.'

'How do you know they stayed all night?'

'Their cars. They sat in the driveway all night. I'd check before I came to work here at eight in the evening and go back after we closed. Car was still there. I went back at five or six in the morning several times. Car still there. I waited till I saw them leave. Six A.M. Never later. Not just casual friends.'

'Can you describe those guys?'

'One was a guy,' said Barbara Henry with a smirk. 'The other was a gal. I saw Saint Betsy kiss her good-bye one morning. That's probably when she saw me and decided I was stalking her.'

18

WEDNESDAY, JANUARY 6—9:10 A.M.

On his desk Wednesday morning Columbo found a memorandum from Tim Mulhaney. Attached to it was a report from the laboratory of the Bureau of Alcohol, Tobacco and Firearms—

BY FAX

To: Detective Timothy Mulhaney, Los Angeles Police
From: Roger Hughes, Technician Bureau of Tobacco, Alcohol and Firearms
Re: Explosive sample # 120-576-0090

The subject sample has been analyzed by chemical and spectrographic analysis. On the basis of the procedures followed, this laboratory is able to state with confidence that the explosive was cyclo-trimethylenetrinitramine $(C_3H_6N_6O_6)$ also known as cyclonite and RDX.

The polymeric binder used to produce the plastic explosive was polyvinyl acetate blended with a synthetic resin. Simply said, the binder was essentially the same material used to manufacture chewing gum. The crystalline $C_3H_6N_6O_6$ was mixed in the binder to form a powerful explosive that would remain safe and stable until detonated by a blasting cap or similar device.

The explosive is entirely common. The binder used is not. We do not suggest that the combination is unique or used by only one chemist, but certainly 'chewing gum' is not the binder of choice of most bomb chemists. In fact BATF can identify only one bomb chemist known to make plastic explosives in this particular way. We must emphasize that we cannot be certain that the man we are about to name is the chemist here, nor have we been able to accumulate enough evidence to convict him of any crime. We have reason to believe, however, that the chemist who produced this bomb was one Harry Lehman, a bomber who spent twenty-two years in federal custody and was released on parole only five years ago. Evidence insufficient on which to base a prosecution suggests that Lehman made bombs this way after his parole.

Unfortunately for your investigation, Harry Lehman was murdered in Las Vegas, Nevada, on December 28. You may find it suggestive that he was killed only three days before this bomb was detonated.

11:32 A.M.

Ai-ling Cooper shook hands with Adrienne Boswell, then sat down across a table from her and pulled a pack of Marlboros from her pocket. She knew Adrienne didn't smoke, so she didn't offer her a cigarette.

'Been a long time, Adrienne. I was told you'd been put on my list of authorized visitors. How'd you work that?'

'A mutual friend did it. Lieutenant

111

Columbo.'

'Columbo—Oh, yeah. I remember you were a friend of his. Still are, huh? You and he, uh . . . you know what I mean?'

Adrienne smiled. 'No way. Even if I threw myself at him—which I was never about to do—I could never have got to first base with him. There's a man who's loyal to wife and home, if ever any man was.'

'Some morning you'll wake up in a motel bed with him and find out at last what I found out to my sorrow: that his innocent act is an act, that he's just setting you up, getting ready to pounce. I ought to know, don't you think? Here I am, thanks to Lieutenant Columbo.'

'He's had every chance,' said Adrienne. 'Anyway, it's too late now. I'm committed to another guy. Anyway—Columbo is a good friend, and that's all.'

'Handsome outfit,' said Ai-ling. She referred to Adrienne's cashmere jacket and skirt of emerald green, the color she favored because it set off nicely against her red hair. 'I've saved money on clothes since I've been here. Anyway—You didn't drive all the way here to talk about Columbo.'

'No. I'm thinking of trying to pick up some of the pieces left behind by Betsy Clendenin. Bill Lloyd let me look at the article she wrote about J. Edgar Hoover. I'm sorry to say this, Ai-ling, but that's old ground that's been plowed pretty thoroughly. She must have had

112

something better than that going.'

'She did, and she didn't give it to me. Naturally, she was holding her best stuff back for the book. She did tell me something about it. She was going to write that Hoover lifted confidential FBI files and had them delivered to Roy Cohn in New York to help him defend himself against the criminal charges that had been brought against him. I imagine it was material he was going to use to blackmail prospective witnesses.'

'What evidence did she have of that?' asked Adrienne.

'I wish I knew. She mentioned the name of a retired FBI agent she was going to interview. She only mentioned him once, and his name just didn't stick in my memory. Believe me, I've tried to remember. After they turn the lights out in this joint, I lie on my cot and try to remember that name. I can't. I can't remember it.'

5:28 P.M.

'Strictly business, Columbo,' said Adrienne. 'Not just a nice social drink at happy hour.' She had been waiting for him in a booth at Fonda la Paloma.

Columbo glanced around. 'Anyway, it's a real nice place,' he said. He sat down opposite her, shrugging out of his raincoat and laying it aside on the seat. 'Sort of beginning to appeal to me.'

'I asked you to come here on a long-shot chance,' she said. 'A real long-shot chance. I drove up and visited Ai-ling Cooper today. You know, of course, that Betsy Clendenin visited her two weeks before the murder. Betsy delivered a manuscript to her, that's going to run as an article in *Glitz*. It's an attack on J. Edgar Hoover. But it's nothing compared to what she was going to have in the book she was writing. She told Ai-ling that she was going to meet with a retired FBI agent and interrogate him about some really damaging stuff. She mentioned the man's name, but Ai-ling can't remember it.'

'That kinda shoots us down, doesn't it?' Columbo asked.

'Well . . . the long-shot chance is that she interviewed him *here*. This was her favorite bar, and she liked to interview people in bars. Even if they didn't drink and loosen up, they relaxed in the casual atmosphere. Better than office interviews, Betsy used to say. Okay. If she interviewed him here, somebody here might remember him.'

Columbo shook his head and smiled wryly. 'Long shot alright.'

'Yeah. We gotta talk to the maitre d'. Say, Columbo, is anybody going to oppose Ai-ling's parole? I understand she comes up for her first hearing in two years. Will the D.A.—?'

'Don't know. Haven't heard anything about it.'

114

'Would the D.A. oppose an application for commutation of sentence?'

'I don't know.'

'Would you write a letter on her behalf?'

'That's a question of departmental policy. I'd hafta talk to Captain Sczciegel, who'd have to talk to the chief. I—'

A waitress came. Adrienne spoke to her. 'Who's in charge here this afternoon?'

'Well—I guess you'd say Eduardo. He's the maitre d'.'

'Tell him we want to talk to him, will you?'

'Is something wrong?'

Adrienne smiled at the girl. 'No, not at all. Just need to talk to him. And bring us two Glenlivets, one on the rocks, one with a splash of soda.'

In a moment the maitre d' came to their booth and asked what he could do for them.

'This is Lieutenant Columbo, Los Angeles Police Department, Homicide. We'd like to ask you a question or two. Can you sit down?'

The maitre d' glanced around, then sat down beside Columbo.

'What's your name, Sir?' Columbo asked him.

'Eduardo Garcia.'

'I understand Miss Betsy Clendenin was a customer of yours and was in here a lot.'

'Yes, Sir. We were very sorry when she was killed.'

'She used to interview people here. For her

writing. I guess you know that.'

'Yes, Sir.'

'About two weeks before she was murdered she may have met a man here. He's a retired man, so we'd hafta figure he'd be sort of old. Also, what he retired from was the FBI. I don't know if retired FBI agents look any different from other people, but that's who he is. Would you happen to remember her being here with a man who might be that retired agent?'

Eduardo Garcia nodded. 'About two weeks before she was murdered she met a man for lunch, man maybe in his seventies. I'm sorry, but that's all I know. He asked for her table, but when she came in she saw him and didn't ask for him, so I didn't hear his name.'

'If I showed you a picture of him, would you remember him?'

'Probably.'

19

THURSDAY, JANUARY 7—7:11A.M.

Dog was happy. He loved nothing better than to scamper on the beach, and this was the best time of day—early in the morning when no young men with too much pride in their odd, hairless muscles strutted and postured on the sand and no young women preened to display their pampered skins. At that time of day the surf ran up the beach and a dog could run at it and bark and order it back, without interference by shrieking children; and the gulls and crabs could work unimpeded in their grimly purposeful searches for bites of food. Mist lay over the scene, and some sort of weird creatures he had never been able to spot belched mournful tones from somewhere out on the water—foghorns, he'd heard someone say.

He would have liked to see a foghorn. Somehow they always eluded him. When the mist cleared, they retreated out to sea, or to the bottom, likely, to save their privacy. Then he, Dog, was left with no companions to play with other than the crabby crabs and the fluttery gulls. He'd caught crabs a few times, but they pinched with their claws, maybe supposing he meant them harm, like maybe to eat them, which he had no interest at all in doing—yucch! And the gulls. If he had managed to catch one, he'd have turned it loose instantly and gone yapping down the beach, sounding his triumph. But they had no sense of fun. Eat one of those? Even a cat wouldn't have done it! They *stank!* Of dead fish!

Of course, there was his master, with his raincoat wrapped around him, puffing on a cigar and watching. The man meant well, Dog supposed. He did, after all, bring him to the beach often. But all he did was sit and watch and smoke. Dog tried to be nice—that is, to entertain him—but his master was not an easy man to entertain. Dog had fetched him a crab once, but his master had only looked pained as he pried the claw apart and tossed the crab toward the water.

Dog had given up on his master. He ignored the foghorns completely, he wouldn't grab crabs, and he wouldn't chase gulls. In fact, he looked like he was tired, though what from would be hard to say. He didn't *do* anything. All he did was sit and watch and sometimes stare out at sea.

Unless maybe it was *think*. Humans did that and seemed to exhaust themselves doing it. They thought too much, worried too much, about nothing that made any difference.

Dog spotted six gulls and charged at them, yapping and wagging his tail. The gulls had no idea how to play. When he got just a little close, they took to wing and glided a scornful distance away, just enough to tire him by running farther after them. So . . . Why bother? They had no sense of fun. Dog trotted to the man in the long coat and shook off water and sand.

'Fella,' said Master. (That was a good word, Dog knew. 'Fella' was a friendly word.) 'How'm I ever going to teach you not to shake on me?'

A little girl stared at Columbo. Maybe eighteen. Maybe only seventeen. She was wearing a white terry beach coat. She left it open for a moment, to let him see the red mini-bikini under it, then closed it and tied the belt. Unfortunately, she was conspicuously stoned, maybe on nothing worse than marijuana, maybe on something worse, since she was here on the beach so early and so obviously woozy.

'The dog don't know much, does he?' she said. It was not a question; it was a comment. 'I mean, like, he doesn't seem to have much smarts, chasin' after gulls he can't catch and . . . and like that.'

'Oh, I don't know. I guess he knows everything he needs to know.'

The girl blinked, then stared. 'That's *deep*,' she said. 'I bet you're right. He knows where to get somethin' to eat, somethin' to drink, a warm place to sleep. What more does a dog need?'

'Love,' said Columbo.

'Hey! You're deep!'

'More like . . . old,' said Columbo.

'No . . . deep. Hey! You could teach a person a lot. I mean, like, you could be somebody's *guru*!'

'How old are you, kiddo?'

'What's the difference?'

'Well, you're out here on the beach very early in the morning, and you're stoned. When'd you get that way? And how?'

'What are you, a Narc? Or a Juvenile?'

'Homicide.'

'Shee-it! Hey . . . Yes, you are! I saw you on the tube! You're that guy . . . What's the name? Columbo! Okay. You gonna cuff me?'

'I haven't got any cuffs, and I haven't got any jurisdiction over you.

'You mean—?'

'You're not my problem.'

The girl stared at him for a moment. Suddenly she sobbed. 'I'm not nobody's problem,' she whispered. 'That's my problem—that I'm just my own problem and nobody else's.'

Columbo glanced at Dog and shook his head. 'Fun's over, Fella,' he said. 'You can come with me if you want to,' he said to the girl. 'Or not if you don't want to. First thing, I've gotta take Dog home. Mrs. Columbo will give us a nice breakfast. Then I gotta go to work. I'll take ya downtown. Not under arrest. Voluntary. When we get it straight how old you are, you go to Juvenile or to detox. You need help. You are somebody's problem.'

The girl shook with sobs. 'I want to be somebody's problem!'

Columbo put an arm around her. 'You got it,' he said. 'You got friends, and you're gonna get help.'

20

The girl turned out to be only sixteen. Columbo delivered her into the custody of a juvenile officer, explaining to the officer how he had found her, also that he had promised her that she was going to experience friendship, not punishment. By the time he had taken care of that and stopped at his desk to see if the morning memos were worth reading, it was time to keep his 10:30 appointment with Marcus Detwiler.

The gilded letters carved into a panel of black marble beside his office doors read—

DETWILER ENTERPRISES, INC.

DETWILER SECURITY SERVICES, INC.

DETWILER INVESTMENT SERVICES, INC.

DETWILER MANAGEMENT SERVICES, INC.

—as if the man couldn't make up his mind what business he was in. Apparently, too, Detwiler was obsessed with black. Stepping into the reception room, Columbo observed that the floors and walls were of black marble, the reception desk was of ebony, and the chairs were upholstered in black leather.

'I'm Lieutenant Columbo, LAPD Homicide. I'm a little early for my appointment.'

The receptionist said nothing but picked up the telephone and told someone 'that homicide detective is here.'

A door opened, and a secretary—dressed in black—came out. 'Mr. Detwiler will see you now,' she said, and gestured that he should go through the door. She led him across her own office, a room with the same decor as the reception area, and knocked softly on another door. It opened, and Marcus Detwiler stepped out and offered his hand.

He was a compact man, barely five-foot-four, with a shiny bullet head, narrow blue eyes, and a broad, toothy smile. He wore a black suit, a white shirt, and a necktie with a pattern dominated by black.

'Lieutenant Columbo! I've heard your name many times but never had the pleasure before. Come in. Have a seat.' He pointed toward a couch upholstered in black leather.

The Detwiler black prevailed in the office decor, but here it was relieved by scores of autographed photographs hanging on the walls and standing in frames on a credenza and on bookshelves. He had photographs with autographs addressed to him of three Presidents of the United States, four United States Senators, maybe a dozen Representatives, two governors, four mayors, and an assortment of entertainment personalities and nondefinable celebrities. A large autographed picture of Jonathan in performance was prominent on one wall.

'Do you enjoy good coffee, Lieutenant? I

have it specially imported from Sweden.'

'I like good coffee,' said Columbo. 'Down at headquarters we get what must be the worst coffee in the world.'

Before he closed the office door, Detwiler told the secretary to bring coffee. Then he sat down on the opposite end of the couch from where Columbo was sitting and turned to face him. 'It's odd,' he said gravely, 'but some people don't seem to care what they eat or drink.'

'Oh, I care what I eat and drink,' Columbo said earnestly. 'For example, I know where you can get the best chili in the city. Also, I do like seafood, anything that comes from the ocean. I have a friend who goes out surf casting. When you eat fish with him, you get *fresh fish*, which is the best.'

'Didn't my secretary offer to hang up your raincoat?'

'Well, I hardly ever—Y'see, I keep stuff in the pockets.'

'I understand. Well, Lieutenant, I imagine I know why you're here. So you just ask me anything you want, and I'll give you the answer.'

'Yes, Sir. Well I went out to see . . . Jonathan. I keep wantin' to call him Mr. Jonathan.'

'You saw him Monday,' Detwiler said simply.

'Right . . . Monday.'

123

'Do you think he's capable of committing a murder?'

Columbo turned down the corners of his mouth and raised his eyebrows. 'Personally? I don't suppose so. But he's capable of giving someone else the orders to do it, and he's got enough money to pay somebody to do it.'

'Then he's a suspect?'

'At this stage, everybody's a suspect—especially people who took a big hit from Miss Clendenin.'

'I won't kid you, Lieutenant Columbo. Jonathan was a multibillion-dollar property until she published. Now—Well, he's a multi*million*-dollar property. I rather imagine I'm a suspect. So let me say this—The death of Betsy Clendenin did Jonathan Enterprises more harm than anything since the original exposé. People will now read her book who hadn't read it before. You want me to name another suspect for you? Take a look at her publisher. Especially, take a look at her paperback publisher. The paperback was to have been out in March. Now it's being rushed forward, to take advantage of the publicity attending her death. My associates and I lost billions to her exposé, and that's not recoverable. Other people stand to profit handsomely from her death.'

The secretary knocked, then entered with the coffee service: a silver pot, creamer, and sugar, with exquisite china. She poured coffee.

Detwiler all but ignored her. He continued. 'If we could have prevented her from making her vicious assault on Jonathan, murder might have suggested itself to us—facetiously speaking, of course—but once it was done her death could not have helped us.'

Columbo tasted the coffee. 'My, this is good coffee! Elegantly served, too. And you've got about the nicest offices I've ever seen.'

'I try to live graciously,' Detwiler said calmly. 'But I've talked on and on and haven't given you a chance to ask your questions. What can I do for you?'

'Well, you've sorta explained it that you'd have had no motive to murder Miss Clendenin,' said Columbo. ' 'Course, losin' a billion dollars would upset some people.'

'I didn't say I wasn't upset. When I first saw her book, I'd have liked to strangle her with my bare hands. But you get over that kind of reaction. Jonathan did make a handsome profit for the men who manage him. Like any other investment, managing Jonathan entailed risks.'

'You, uh, sort of *created* him, huh?'

'Actually, he created himself. We packaged and sold his creation. We knew his problems. He's not a very nice man, Lieutenant. Unfortunately, what Miss Clendenin told about him was mostly true. We concealed it as long as possible but knew all along it would come out someday.'

125

Columbo sipped coffee and nodded. 'The fact is, the man's not terribly bright, is he?'

Detwiler smiled, then chuckled. 'You got it. You figured it out.'

'You talk about managing him. I guess he had to have a manager, didn't he?'

'A management team. Yes. We managed him. Still do.'

'Well, uh, I don't want to take too much of your time. I can see you're a busy man, with lots of interests goin'.'

'My time is your time, Lieutenant Columbo. What you're doing is important.'

Columbo scratched his chin. 'I like to think so. A man likes to think that what he does with his life is worth somethin'.'

'I admire people like you. You lead an enviable life.'

'Well, thank ya.' Columbo stood. 'Sometimes I think I'd like to have an office like this. Then I get to thinkin', no matter how nice the office, I'm really not the kind of guy that can work all day in an office. So—Well—Thanks for the coffee.'

'I'll have my secretary send you a pound of it.'

'That's very kind of ya, Sir. Very kind. So. I'll be goin'.'

'Call on me anytime. It's been a pleasure.'

Detwiler rose and walked toward the door.

'Oh, Sir. There is one more little thing I'd like to ask. Probably got nothing to do with

126

anything, but it's one of those little things that'll prey on my mind if I don't get the answer to the question.'

'What question, Lieutenant?'

'Well, Sir, you and your associates manage Jonathan. He's not too bright and can't manage for himself. So who managed to get Kitty and her mother to Brazil? Did you and your associates arrange that?'

Detwiler laughed. 'You're a shrewd one, Lieutenant Columbo. Alright, yes. We did arrange for Kitty and her mother to live in Brazil. I don't deny it. At that point we were protecting a billion-dollar property.'

'Then Penny? Penelope Kent? And her father. Are they in Brazil, too?'

Detwiler's smile snapped into a dark frown. 'I don't *know*. I know Betsy Clendenin implied something, but I don't know anything about them. I didn't make any 'arrangements' for them.'

Columbo nodded. 'I thank ya again. I'm glad to have that little point explained. It puts my mind at rest on it.'

12:18 P.M.

Martha Zimmer sat beside Columbo on a bench in Pershing Square and munched on a hot dog wrapped in paper. They had bought hot dogs and Pepsis from a cart vendor.

'Mr. Detwiler talked about good food,' said

127

Columbo, 'and it gave me a sudden hunger for a hot dog boiled on a cart. This cart guy makes good kraut, too. Kraut's what makes this hot dog special. Sorry you didn't order any on yours.'

'Everyone to his own taste,' Martha said through a mouthful of hot dog.

'This case is gettin' interesting. There's something I'd like for you to check up on for me. Take a look at Miss Clendenin's book about Jonathan, the part where she talks about his playin' around with little girls. Actually, don't read it if you're squeamish.'

'I *have* read it, Columbo. You're probably the only man in Los Angeles that hadn't read it until now.'

'Well . . . I usually don't take much interest in that sorta stuff. What celebrity types do doesn't much interest me. Like, I'd never seen a Regina concert or tape before she got murdered. Anyway, Miss Clendenin says that Kitty, the girl who told her so much, is living in some town in Brazil, 'way up the Amazon, so is completely out of touch. Miss Clendenin located her, but she said she never could find Penny Kent. I—'

'I remember. I read that.'

'Mr. Detwiler didn't like it much when I mentioned that to him. What I'd appreciate it if you'd do is go over to Juvenile and see what they have on Penelope Kent and her father Edward.'

128

'Juvenile files are confidential, you know,' said Martha.

'Not when you're investigating a possible homicide.'

Martha frowned. She lowered the can from which she had been about to take a sip of Pepsi. 'You *serious*?'

'Well, let's look at it *this* way. Mr. Detwiler made a big point of sayin' his group would have had no motive to kill Miss Clendenin, because she'd done the damage and it couldn't be undone. But Jonathan was a billion-dollar property. If the Kents, father and daughter, had got out of line, that could've damaged the billion-dollar property. They protected their investment by payin' off the Lockharts, plain enough. But what did they do about Penelope and Edward Kent? I hear Detwiler plays rough.'

'I've heard that too. Damnit, it's starting to rain!'

1:51 P.M.

'Hiya, Ben!' Columbo said to FBI agent Ben Parnell. 'How's it goin'?'

He was reluctant to ask Ben Parnell how it was going, because he knew Parnell would tell him.

'Not good, Columbo. Not good. Y'know, they just keep piling it on us. I mean, like, in this office we got three agents less than we had

129

two years ago, and the case load is up eighteen percent. And of course the damned hemorrhoids still pain me, and my migraines are back.' He shook his head. 'I'm gonna retire and move to Arizona.'

He was Columbo's age but looked older. His yellow hair, always thin, was all but gone except above his ears and around the back of his neck. His complexion was pink. He wore silver-framed glasses.

'Sorry to hear it, Ben. Me, I've thought about retirement. I've got enough years in. But what'd I do with myself. Mrs. C says I'd drive her nuts, sittin' around the house. She'd want me to take courses at one of the universities, learn art or literature or psychology or somethin'. I don't know. I think I'll keep pluggin' away while my health is good.'

'That's one thing you've got goin' for you: good health—though you really ought to get more exercise,' Parnell said lugubriously. 'Anyway, what can the FBI do for the LAPD today?'

I need to talk to ya about retired agents living in the L.A. area,' said Columbo. 'There may be nothing in what I've got in mind, but it might be helpful, too. You guys keep files on retired guys?'

'Yeah. Sometimes they've got information we can really use. I guess there'd be fifty retired agents living in the county, more in the counties around here.'

130

'Can you give me a list of them, Ben?'

'Don't see why not. Sure. Yeah, I can give you a list. Can I ask what for?'

'I wanta use it to see if it jogs somebody's memory.'

21

FRIDAY, JANUARY 8—11:01 A.M.

Ai-ling Cooper sat down opposite Columbo at a table in the prison visiting room. He hadn't seen her for a long time, and he was sorry to see that the years had not been good to her. She was heavier than he remembered, and obviously she was no longer bothering to style herself. Well—Actually, there was nothing wrong with her that couldn't be remedied in a few weeks after her release. He made a mental note to find an occasion to see her when she'd been out a couple of months. He'd bet she'd look a lot like her old self.

'I'm damned if I can think of a reason why I should see you,' she said. 'My travel agent. This is one hell of a reservation you arranged for me. You ever been where you didn't know what day of the week it was, 'cause it didn't make any difference? I can't think of a single reason why I should talk to *you*.'

'I can't think of a reason why you should, either,' said Columbo.

'But I didn't refuse,' she said, shaking out a

cigarette and lighting it with a paper match. I suppose there's something I can do for you, or you wouldn't be here. You were not a man to waste his time, as I remember.'

'Maybe it's somethin' *I* can do for you. Adrienne Boswell tells me you lie awake nights tryin' to think of the name of the retired FBI agent Miss Clendenin mentioned to you. Well, I got here a list of retired agents livin' in the Los Angeles area. Would you look over the list and see if any of them is the man she mentioned.'

Ai-ling nodded. He handed her the list prepared for him by Ben Parnell, and she glanced down it, shaking her head grimly. Suddenly she stopped. 'Alright. Yeah. Here we go. Kloss. I'd swear the name was Kloss. Unusual name, huh? Yeah, she said she was going to see a man named Kloss.'

'I thank ya, Mrs. Cooper-Svan. That takes a load off your mind, and it may help to take one off mine.'

'Any time, Lieutenant Columbo,' she said dispiritedly. 'Any time I can help the LAPD . . .'

4:49 P.M.

'*Fritz Kloss!*'

'That's the name she picked out,' said Columbo.

Ben Parnell laughed. 'If she hadn't died in that explosion, she have died during the

132

interview—of boredom. Fritz Kloss could bore the stripes off a zebra.'

'Anyway, that's the name she remembers. I'd like to show a picture of him to a possible witness. You got a picture you can lend me, Ben? Or a group of pictures?'

'Sure. But—Fritz is an old nut. He comes in here every couple of months and stands around shaking his head. He was an agent when Hoover was in charge and he's still got the J. Edgar Hoover mania.'

'Mania?'

'J. Edgar Hoover was a *nut*, Columbo. An egomaniacal nut. The agency is lucky— damned lucky—to have survived his fumbling mismanagement. The man was a colossal egomaniac, a hatemonger, a—Well, there's no awe of him anymore, except I suppose in the minds of a few addled old fellows like Fritz. He's always sniffing around and telling us it wouldn't have been done that way when the 'Director'—as he always calls him—was in charge.'

'Did he work out of this office?'

'He did after Hoover died. Once John Edgar was gone, the new directors shifted a lot of the Hoover maniacs to regional offices. Los Angeles got Kloss. Before that, he spent most of his career in what Hoover called SOG— Seat of Government, meaning Washington. He was personally acquainted with the man. Ol' Fritz would have licked J. Edgar Hoover's shoes if Hoover had asked him.'

'How close a friend, ya figure?'

'So far as anyone has ever been able to figure out, J. Edgar Hoover had only one friend in his life: Clyde Tolson. So Kloss wouldn't have been a friend. But from the way he talks, I'm certain he was a Hoover toady. To old Fritz, Hoover was a *saint*—a plaster saint, I'd call him, but a real saint to Fritz.'

'This is a big help, Ben. I'd appreciate that photo. Like to take it with me, if I can.'

'You aren't telling me Fritz Kloss blew away Betsy Clendenin?'

Columbo shook his head. 'I couldn't say that. But he may be a lead.'

Parnell shook his head emphatically. 'Not Kloss. It wouldn't be in him.'

'Yeah? Well . . . let me change the subject. Did you ever hear of a guy named Harry Lehman?'

Parnell shook his head.

'The BATF says he may have built the bomb. It was like bombs he built.'

'Like a computer check on him?'

'That might be helpful. I'd appreciate it.'

Ben Parnell turned to his desktop computer terminal, which was linked by telephone to the FBI main files in Washington. 'Lehman? L-E-H-M-A-N? Harry.'

'That's what they say.'

Parnell tapped keys, then leaned back and waited. 'Okay. Here we go—*Hey, Columbo!*

134

The man's dead! Murdered on December 28. Looks like a Mafia hit. Shot. Executed. And . . . Let's see—Hey, hey! Guess who sent him to Leavenworth for twenty-two years. Fritz Kloss. There y'go. Fritz sent him up on a tough charge. How 'bout that?'

7:22 P.M.

'Ya said you wanted to know what Mrs. Cooper-Svan said. Ya said you wanted to be in on anything that came out of it. Well . . . When you say things like that, you get to work late.'

Adrienne sat down opposite him in a booth in Fonda la Paloma. She had come from an indoor tennis court and was wearing her tennis whites. She ordered Scotch for both of them. 'You been a busy boy today?'

I went to see Mrs. Cooper-Svan—'

'She'd like to drop the 'Svan,' Columbo.'

'I went to see Mrs. Cooper. I had a list of retired FBI agents who lived around here. She recognized one of the names. He's a man in his seventies by the name of Frederick Kloss, called Fritz. The current FBI guys think he's something of a nut.'

'Well, that's what you want if you're looking for a man who committed a murder by blowing someone to pieces.'

'I got his picture here. I thought we'd show it to Eduardo.'

Eduardo Garcia, the maitre d', came to the

135

table. Columbo laid out four photographs. 'Recognize any of those?' he asked.

Garcia stared thoughtfully at them. 'That one,' he said, pointing at the second photo.

'Who is he?'

'He's the man who had lunch with Miss Clendenin.'

22

SATURDAY, JANUARY 9—9:49 A.M.

Columbo walked into Pittocco's, where his new jacket would be ready.

The handsome, dark-haired woman who had waited on him came out and greeted him. 'Lieutenant Columbo! How nice to see you. Your jacket is ready.'

'Ah, good. Mrs. C wants me to wear it to a party we're goin' to tonight.'

'Wonderful! Are you sure your slacks are—'

'Well, Mrs. Columbo did make a point of havin' a pair of dark-brown slacks, practically new, drycleaned this week.'

'Maybe you need a shirt. You did buy a very nice tie. A new white shirt would complete the outfit.'

'Well, I—I don't know. I'm kinda hard on my clothes. I've got lots of shirts—'

'If you'll forgive my saying so, the one you've got on won't do real justice to the jacket and tie.'

136

'Yeah . . . Yeah, this shirt has seen better times.'

'Let me show you a white dress shirt.'

Another fifty dollars. He didn't know if he wanted to come to this store again or not. The woman wasn't pushy like the guys in the outlet stores where he bought his clothes, but she some way did manage to get him to spend fifty dollars he hadn't expected to spend.

2:00 P.M.

Walter Mahaffey had sent the two hundred typescript pages that Betsy Clendenin had submitted to him. They arrived on Thursday. Columbo was resolved to read them this Saturday afternoon.

Some of the material was very interesting—

The word loyalty mean nothing to J. Edgar Hoover. An agent obeyed even his direct personal orders at his peril.

In May, 1962, for example, the Director called on New York agent Wilson Harvey and ordered him to install listening devices in a hotel room soon to be occupied by Meyer Lansky. Agent Harvey arranged for the microphones to be installed and for wires to be run to an FBI listening post on the floor below. For weeks the FBI taped every word spoken by Meyer Lansky, mostly casual conversation with his wife.

One night while watching a television documentary on organized crime, Lansky remarked to his wife that organized crime was bigger than U.S. Steel. Harvey sent a transcript of that conversation directly to Hoover, who leaked it to one of his favorite journalists, David Kinder. A few nights later, Lansky, still fascinated with television reports on organized crime, was startled to hear himself quoted by Kinder—'Why, organized crime is bigger than U.S. Steel!'

It was obvious that the remark could only have gotten loose through a bug in Lansky's room. Lansky searched the room thoroughly and found the microphones. The next day, Lansky's attorneys called on Attorney General Robert Kennedy.

Bugging and wiretapping were in ill repute at that moment. Congressional hearings were being held on a bill to limit the practices. So Kennedy was sensitive to the complaint from Meyer Lansky. He took the matter up with J. Edgar Hoover.

So what did Hoover do? He fired Wilson Harvey. He fired him, saying the FBI did not countenance such techniques—this in spite of the fact that he personally had ordered the bugging.

Columbo went to the refrigerator and pulled out a can of beer. He read on—

THE FBI term for bugging was 'misur,' meaning 'microphone surveillance.' The list of people subjected to misurs reads like a <u>Who's Who</u>. It will surprise no one, probably, to learn that Marilyn Monroe's home and many of her hotel suites were bugged. Director Hoover absolutely lusted for a misur tape that would catch one of the Kennedy brothers having intimacy with Marilyn. Unhappily for him, his lust was never satisfied.

In the case of Dr. Martin Luther King, Jr. he had more success. The misur transcripts of Dr. King's conversations do not prove that the famous black leader indulged himself outside his marriage, but they were 'evidence' enough for Director Hoover, who believed that black men are more eminently endowed than white men, which results in libidinousness that white men can never hope to match.

The Director, as his surviving acolytes persist in calling him, was an obsessive racist—among the many other defects in his character. It was only under heavy pressure that he allowed the FBI to employ black agents; and when it did he constantly referred to them as 'coons' and refused to allow them to have any significant assignments.

Columbo finished his beer, took half an hour off to go out in the driveway and wipe dust from his Peugeot, and opened another beer. Mrs. Columbo was doing her usual Saturday afternoon shopping. Their daughter was coming for dinner that night, and Mrs. C was going to serve lasagna.

He flipped through some pages that didn't much interest him, then came on this—

In 1968 Director Hoover implemented an agreement he had made with the Polemarco crime family of Los Angeles. Frank, 'Frankie the Pole' Polemarco was about to go on trial in federal court in Los Angeles on charges of murder and kidnapping. Suddenly an essential witness, one Bernie Levin, had a change of heart and decided not to testify. He could not be persuaded to testify. Why? It was not, as the D.A. supposed, because of threats Levin had received from Polemarco's crime family. No. The reason was that attorneys for the defense had been given access to confidential FBI files that implicated Levin in espionage activities on behalf of the Soviet Union, in the late 1940's and early 'fifties. The evidence was inconclusive at best, but it would have been immensely damaging to Levin to have it made public. He feared deportation to Estonia, where he was born.

Without Levin's testimony the prosecution of the case against Polemarco could not go on.

Why did J. Edgar Hoover release secret files to the Polemarco defense lawyers? It was payment per an agreement between them. For their part of the deal, the Polemarcos obtained and turned over to him some grainy old sixteen-millimeter film of a movie actress whose name I will protect. It was a 'stag' film, made in the 'forties. Hoover had wanted the film for two reasons—one for the titillation of seeing the famous star in the most intimate of acts, two because her husband was seriously considering a campaign for a Senate seat. Faced with the Director's suggestion that the film would have to be made public, the

141

husband withdrew.

Venal as this was, it was nothing compared to the nefarious deal Director Hoover made with the notorious sleazeball shyster Roy Cohn—of which more, much more, later.

PART FOUR

'Look at him. He doesn't comb his hair, he dresses shoddily, he walks around in a slouch with a stub of a cigar in his mouth. The man has no self-respect . . . This fellow Columbo has no self-respect.'

—FRITZ KLOSS

'You show me a man that doesn't wear a hat, and I'll show you a man with no respect for himself!'

—JOHN EDGAR HOOVER

23

MONDAY, JANUARY 11—7:33 A.M.

Fritz Kloss sat over his breakfast as usual. His jacket hung on another chair, but he wore his vest, white shirt, and tie. He sipped his coffee and ate his bacon and eggs as he scanned the Los Angeles *Times*.

'Fritz . . . You let me sleep! I'd have made your breakfast.'

He stood, kissed Meredith, and poured her a cup of coffee. 'You and I,' he said, 'are creatures of habit. It's mine, for too many years, to get up early every morning, make my own breakfast, and read my morning paper. It's yours to sleep as late as you can, have coffee, and run. One of the best things about this relationship is that we accommodate each other.'

'Well . . . '

She sat down. She was wearing a black bra and black bikini panties. She had given her hair a few strokes of her brush, but she had not put on any makeup.

'You really can't drive me down this morning?' she asked.

'I'm afraid not, honey. I agreed to meet Lieutenant Columbo, the LAPD detective who's investigating the death of Betsy. I should've made him come later, so I could drive you to the studio.'

'No big deal,' said Meredith. 'What's the detective want?'

'I don't know, really. And, frankly, I don't give a damn. When a homicide detective asks to interview you, you do it. But I don't know anything he could possibly want to know. Anyway, the man's no detective.'

'What makes you say that?'

'I've seen him on television. So have you. Look at him. He doesn't comb his hair, he dresses shoddily, he walks around in a slouch with a stub of a cigar in his mouth. The man has no self-respect. That was one of the things the Director most emphatically insisted on: that an agent have self-respect, which manifests itself in the way he appears and handles himself. This fellow Columbo has no self-respect.'

9:15 A.M.

When Columbo went to see Frederick Kloss, he wore his new jacket and shirt and tie. The FBI had long put big emphasis on appearance, and it might not hurt if Kloss saw him from the first as a man of dignity. And as a proper policeman. He carried his revolver in its holster under his left arm. Of course, Kloss didn't need to know his bullets were in the car.

The man lived well. Columbo had checked

146

him out a bit. After he retired from the FBI in 1974, he had gone into real estate, and Frederick Kloss Realtors, Incorporated was still a big business. Though he was retired from that, too, it probably paid him dividends or a generous pension.

The man answered his door dressed in a dark-gray vested suit, white shirt, and narrow maroon-and-black necktie. 'Lieutenant Columbo. Come in.'

'Why, thank ya. Maybe this isn't a convenient time for you. I mean, were you gettin' ready to go out?'

Fritz Kloss smiled. 'I don't lounge around in khakis and sweatshirts, Lieutenant. I've had a lifelong habit of dressing each day.'

'You know, I'm that way myself. When I'm mowin' the grass or workin' on my car, I'll wear grubbies, as ya might say; but I don't feel comfortable about it other times. Maybe it's the discipline of police work. Y'suppose?'

'Old habit of wearing something that will cover your sidearm,' said Fritz. 'Can I serve us some coffee?'

'Very kind of ya. Uh—Do you, uh, *still* carry your sidearm?'

Fritz smiled. 'Oh, no. I put it aside when I retired and haven't carried a gun since. Have a seat. I'll bring us some coffee.'

While the man was gone, Columbo looked around his home. From the look of things, Mr. Kloss had an obsession with neatness. Even the magazines on his coffee table—*National Geographic, U.S. News & World Report, American Rifleman*—were piled with their edges parallel to the edges of the table. His morning newspaper was carefully folded and looked as if it had not been opened or read.

Fritz returned. 'Cream and sugar?'

'No, thanks. Black.'

'You've come to ask me what I know about the death of Betsy Clendenin.'

'Yes, Sir. I would like to talk about that, if ya don't mind.'

'What connects me to her death?'

'She was workin' on a book about the FBI. She told somebody she was gonna interview you. Then she did interview you, at Fonda la Paloma. Y'see, I don't think she got killed by somebody who wanted revenge for what she'd exposed about them. That damage was done and couldn't be reversed. My idea is, she was killed by somebody who wanted to prevent her from publishing something in the future. We know she was working on a book about J. Edgar Hoover and the FBI. We also know she had some very unkind things to say. I have to wonder if somebody with some connection to the FBI didn't—'

'FBI people don't murder people, Lieutenant,' Fritz said coldly. 'We're on the other side.'

'Oh, I have no doubt of that, Sir. I just wondered if anything had come to your

148

attention that would suggest—'

'No, Lieutenant. No one who speaks to me made any suggestion that the woman should be murdered—if that's what you want to know.'

'She did interview you?'

'She sure did. Lieutenant Columbo, did you ever meet Betsy Clendenin?'

'No, I never did.'

'An aggressive woman. A careless journalist, not meticulous about evidence. She was not a credit to her profession. She was simply collecting every discredited slander that was ever raised against the Director and was going to publish them all again. All she had in mind was the money she could make from it.'

'Did you try to talk her out of it?' Columbo asked.

'I did. But she was not interested in the truth.'

'Which was?'

'Which was what, Lieutenant?'

'What was the truth?'

'The truth, Lieutenant Columbo, is that J. Edgar Hoover was one of the finest public servants this nation has ever produced. I can't say I'm sorry her book will never appear.' He shrugged. 'On the other hand, she invited me to a party, and I went and enjoyed myself very much. Indeed, she introduced me to the woman I'm having a very friendly relationship with.'

149

'Where was this party, Sir?'

'At her house. She had, I suppose, about twenty guests. And she introduced me to Meredith Nelson, the television actress. She did me a real favor.'

'Did she say anything to you about being threatened, or anything like that?'

'Yes. She said she was threatened all the time—which she seemed to find somewhat amusing. She carried a gun in her purse, incidentally.'

'Did she say she'd been threatened specifically because she was working on the Hoover book?'

'No, not specifically.'

Columbo pressed his hands together in front of his face. 'I'm takin' your time,' he said.

'Not at all. I'm happy to help any way I can. I wish I could do more.'

'Well—if ya get any ideas, let me know. I could use help from an experienced investigator like you. Y'see, I'm not a genius. The only way I know to find out who murdered somebody is just to accumulate all the facts I can and try to make some kinda sense out of them. It's a lot of work. I just work hard. Sometimes I wish I could get what they call insights, but insights just don't come to me; I just have to do the work.'

'That's how it always was with me, Lieutenant,' Fritz said tolerantly. 'That's how the Director wanted it done: by painstaking hard work.'

'Yes, Sir. So, I thank ya.' Columbo stood. 'Thanks for the coffee, too. It's very good.'

Fritz rose and walked to the door with Columbo. 'Call on me any time, if you think of any way I can be of help.'

'Yes, Sir. I sure will.' Columbo stepped outside, where abruptly he stopped, just as Fritz was closing the door. 'Oh, say, Sir, there is just one other little thing I meant to ask you. Prob'ly isn't important, but—Did you ever hear of a man named Harry Lehman?'

Fritz Kloss turned down the corners of his mouth and shook his head. 'No, Lieutenant. I don't think I've ever heard that name in my life.'

'Well, thank ya again. It was just a long shot, that you might have known the man sometime.'

Fritz shook his head, and Columbo walked toward his car.

24

10:47 A.M.

'I hope this isn't inconvenient.'

'Not at all. Come in.'

Linda Semon was the young woman Walter Mahaffey had mentioned as having done research work for Betsy Clendenin. She was a tiny, mousy girl, probably not yet twenty-five

151

years old. Her hair was short, cut in an almost mannish style, she wore round, plastic-rimmed spectacles, and if she used makeup, she had not yet applied it this morning. She was dressed like a schoolgirl: in a pleated skirt, blue-and-green plaid, with a white blouse closed at her throat with a gold pin.

Her small apartment was almost as neat as Kloss's, though it was more imaginatively furnished. Her computer sat on a table made by laying a piece of plywood across two milk crates. Her walls were decorated with color photographs, one of which was of Betsy Clendenin capering in the surf. As he glanced at the several pictures, Columbo could see that Linda Semon had taken them herself—except for one which was of herself and Betsy, taken probably that same day on the beach.

'Sit down, Lieutenant. Make yourself comfortable. I suppose I'm a suspect.'

'No. I hadn't thought of you as a suspect. Just as a possible witness, just as someone who might have some facts I could use.'

'You haven't heard about the insurance policy. Neither had I until Wednesday, when Betsy's lawyer called and told me I was the beneficiary of a half-million-dollar life insurance policy Betsy had bought a couple of months ago. Also, it seems I'm in her will. I inherit half her net estate. Also, I inherit all her notes, tapes, and disks—everything related to unfinished work.'

152

Columbo nodded. 'Uh, I guess you were something more than just a research assistant.'

Linda nodded and smiled. 'Who told you I was her research assistant?'

'Mr. Mahaffey, her publisher.'

Linda's smile faded as she shook her head. 'Do I have to explain?'

'No, Ma'am.'

'Oh, I did do research for Betsy. I was a sort of assistant to her, and she did pay me—generously—but our relationship was personal: very, very personal. I miss her terribly.'

'I have to ask you a question, Miss Semon. Did you sometimes stay all night at Miss Clendenin's house?'

'Yes. And she sometimes stayed here.'

'Do you know if anyone else ever stayed overnight at Miss Clendenin's house?'

'Doug. Douglas Smith. Betsy was a woman of catholic tastes, Lieutenant Columbo. She left him $50,000. He's more than a little annoyed about what I got. He thought she was going to leave him as much as she left me. He's not very bright. Betsy didn't prize him for his brains.'

'Should I think of him as a suspect?' Columbo asked.

Linda shook her head. 'I don't.'

'Lemme change the subject. Does the name Frederick Kloss mean anything to you?'

'Of course it does. You want a suspect?

153

There's a suspect. Betsy thought he had something to do with the delivery of confidential FBI files to Roy Cohn.'

'Why did she think J. Edgar Hoover sent confidential FBI files to Roy Cohn?'

'Hoover had his agenda. Have you heard about what he did in the Polemarco case?'

'I read about it Saturday afternoon. Mr. Mahaffey sent me a couple hundred pages of what Miss Clendenin had written so far.'

'Okay. He helped Polemarco blackmail a witness who would have given damaging testimony against him in a murder trial. He did that because—Well, you read it. Because he wanted a piece of film. He helped Roy Cohn blackmail witnesses because he and Cohn were lovers. Cohn had a country home in Greenwich, Connecticut, at the time, and Hoover used to go there incognito. There were never more than three of them in the house: Cohn, Hoover, and Tolson. When Cohn died, women's underwear in outlandish sizes was found in a closet. It was for Director Hoover. He had worn it.'

'How did Miss Clendenin find out about all this?'

'A lot of agents, active and retired, hated Hoover's guts—for very good reasons, incidentally. When the word got out that Betsy was going to write a book about J. Edgar Hoover, she had to make them get in line to talk to her. She had tapes of many interviews.

All that was destroyed in the explosion.'

'*All* of it?'

'No. Actually not all of it. I had a couple of tape cartridges here that I was going to transcribe for Betsy. They survived. I haven't figured out quite what to do with them. I haven't had the heart to transcribe them. Her voice is on them, you understand. I—'

'Let me make you a suggestion. Off the record. It isn't exactly right for me to do this. But . . . uh, some of what Miss Clendenin was doing may get picked up by another writer, Miss Adrienne Boswell. You ever hear of her?'

'She was a friend of Betsy's.'

'Right. So, if it's okay with you—and *only* if it's okay with you—I'll suggest to Adrienne that she call you.'

'Well, uh . . . That's okay with me, Lieutenant. I'll talk to her, anyway.'

'And one other little thing, Miss Semon. Did it ever occur to you that you might be in danger?'

Linda Semon shook her head. 'I don't think so. Betsy's been dead ten days, and you just now got around to me. A lot of people knew I did research and other work for her, but nobody could know I have those two tapes. The whole world knew what Betsy was doing and what evidence she had. She talked about it on television. But nobody knows much about me.'

'If you have any reason to call 911—like, if

you think you hear a prowler or you think you're being followed—tell the 911 operator that Lieutenant Columbo promised you quick help and protection if you should need it.'

'Betsy bought me a pistol. She took me to a range and taught me to shoot.'

'Callin' the cops is better. Believe me, it's better.'

12:43 P.M.

'Columbo! My god, look at the new threads!'

He was meeting Adrienne for lunch as much to let her see his new clothes as for any other reason.

'I was supposed to buy a raincoat, but I couldn't see any point in that when it's still got so much good service in it. So I had the gift certificate and decided to buy this jacket instead. Then the woman sold me a fifty-dollar necktie and a fifty-dollar shirt. Then when I got the shirt home I found out I had to have cuff links. Lucky I had some. Lucky I could find 'em. They were my father's. Look at 'em. They're little racks of pool balls. See? My father loved to play pool. I inherited that from him. And these cuff links. They're real gold, my mother said. I never had the heart to let a jeweler look at them. If they're not real gold, I don't want to know it.'

'They're beautiful,' said Adrienne.

'Well—Here's a phone number.' He handed

156

her a pencilled note. 'That's Linda Semon. She was Miss Clendenin's research assistant. She was somethin' more besides, I might as well tell ya. She's got a coupla cartridges of tape, with some retired FBI guy on there spillin' his guts.'

'Is she in danger?' Adrienne asked.

'Not if we keep her secret.'

25

MONDAY, JANUARY 11—2:06 P.M.

'Columbo! Man, that's handsome!'

'Hey, Columbo! Got a new girlfriend?'

'Tailored so your sidearm fits under there, absolutely out of sight. First class, Columbo!'

Martha Zimmer, who was walking beside Columbo, grinned and winked at Captain Sczciegel.

'I don't think I'm gonna wear it to the office anymore,' Columbo groused. 'It's embarrassin' to—'

'Hey! Your *friends*, man. Payin' you a compliment. That's what it is, a compliment. Your new threads are beautiful, Columbo. My compliments to Mrs. C. I assume she picked it out.'

'Nah. I picked it out myself—with some help, actually, from the woman that works in the store.'

'Now, if you'd just get a new raincoat.'

'Why, when my raincoat's got so much good service left in it? Listen. If I got a new raincoat, I'd hafta be like I am with this jacket—like, afraid to put a ballpoint pen in the pocket, for fear it'll leak and stain. I rubbed the gun all over with a towel, to make sure it doesn't have any oil on it that could get loose and—'

'I get ya, Columbo. But it is a handsome jacket.'

'Well, I thank ya. We goin' to find out anything?'

'I'm not sure.'

They were on their way to Juvenile Division, where they were to be briefed on the case of Penelope Kent.

Sergeant Margaret Phillips was an attractive blond woman, maybe forty years old. She wore a black skirt and a white blouse. Her badge as a police officer was displayed on a fold of a leather case in her breast pocket. She invited the two detectives from Homicide to sit down facing her desk. She had a small private office. She interviewed a lot of children and parents.

'We *could* transfer this file from Juvenile to Homicide,' she said immediately. 'I have a strong suspicion that Penny Kent is dead.'

'Whatta ya base that on?' Columbo asked.

Sergeant Phillips ran her left hand over her forehead and down over her left eye, as if she had a headache. 'I'm sure you know, Lieutenant, that we just don't have the

158

resources to search the whole world, or even the whole country, for a missing juvenile. We put out a bulletin on Kitty Lockhart, and we didn't find her. There's only so much we can do. Betsy Clendenin went looking for Kitty. She's only got one missing kid to look for, we've got thousands; and she found her. But she couldn't find Penny. Or her father. The Kents just disappeared off the face of the earth.'

'People can do that,' said Martha.

'Betsy Clendenin's Jonathan book came out in September,' Sergeant Phillips went on. 'That was the first time that Juvenile Division heard of the goings-on at Xanadu. The place is outside our jurisdiction, of course, but the two girls mentioned in the book lived in LA, so we went to see them. Both of them were gone, disappeared.'

'How long before?' Columbo asked.

'Couple of weeks, maybe three weeks, before we went to interview them.'

'Well . . . Still doesn't prove they're dead,' Columbo said skeptically, though he was beginning to accept the sergeant's judgment.

'Let me tell you a little more,' said Sergeant Phillips, again pressing her hand to her forehead. 'When Kitty Lockhart and her mother disappeared, they packed a few personal things. When we got a warrant and looked into the apartment where the Kents had lived, everything was in place, so far as anyone could tell. If Kent had more shirts and slacks and socks and underwear than were in his closet and drawers, he must have bought them the way Imelda Marcos bought shoes. If a teenage girl had more clothes than were left in Penny's room—'

I get your point,' said Columbo. 'Excuse me. Do you have a headache?'

'I have migraines,' she said quietly.

'Anything we can do for ya? We can drop this for now and come back later.'

Sergeant Phillips shook her head. 'What you can do for me is close the door and not think I'm weird if I stretch out on my back on the floor. That helps.'

Columbo closed the door, and Sergeant Phillips did just what she said she wanted to do—she pulled a cushion off her chair and put it under her head as she lay on her back on the floor of her office. She closed her eyes.

'You see a doctor for that?' Columbo asked.

'Lieutenant, I've seen a *dozen* doctors for this. I have a headache about one day a week. Hey, I can handle it, especially when I'm talking to somebody sympathetic enough to let me lie down and close my eyes. I have a theory about what happened to Penny Kent. It's a theory, alright? But it's my theory. Bea Lockhart was an addict and sold her daughter to get her daily fix. Edward Kent was not an addict; he was just a completely corrupt man who saw his daughter as a way to pick up some important cash. After a while he thought he saw a way to pick up a hell of a lot more—by blackmailing Jonathan, that is by blackmailing the Jonathan organization. Jonathan was still a superstar when Kent tried that. The guys couldn't take a risk on Kent. They killed him and his daughter. Okay? Theory.'

'Persuasive . . .' murmured Martha.

'Miss Clendenin arranged to have the disappearance of Penny Kent run on the TV show 'America's Most Wanted,' which means her face and her father's face were seen on millions of television screens all over the country. The show got half a dozen calls from people who claimed to have seen the Kents, or one of them. Police in six towns checked those out. In every case it turned out that the girl someone thought was Penny wasn't Penny, and the man someone thought was Edward Kent was not Edward Kent.'

'I gotta strong feeling you're right, Sergeant,' said Columbo. 'I'm not sure it's enough to justify transferring the case to Homicide.'

'As a homicide case it gets a whole lot more attention.'

'You got a point. I'll talk to the captain about it.'

3:02 P.M.

'Why not?' was Captain Sczciegel's reaction.

161

'At least we can say we got a possible suspect. Uh . . . not Jonathan himself, right? Detwiler. Somebody in his organization.'

'Cap'n, Jonathan is *pitiful*. He couldn't hurt anybody if he wanted to. But Detwiler has got thugs on his payroll. He admitted to me, without any hesitation, that he arranged for Kitty Lockhart and her mother to go to Brazil. When I asked him about Penny Kent, he turned hard and said he didn't know anything about her.'

'The trail will be cold,' the captain said. If Penny and her father were murdered, it had to be in . . . what? August?'

'August, probably,' said Martha Zimmer.

'Of course, when the word goes out that we have transferred the file to Homicide, new sources of information may appear,' said Captain Semiegel.

'We got another suspect, Captain. A retired FBI agent by the name of Kloss.'

'Fritz Kloss? I know him. What in the world would make you think he could have killed Betsy Clendenin?'

'Kind of a thin case,' said Columbo. 'Until this morning, when he lied to me. Now I gotta follow up on him, whether I like it or not.'

'You could really shoot yourself in the foot, Columbo. Going after a retired agent of the Federal Bureau of Investigation. I mean—'

'I'm with ya, Cap'n. Gotta be really sure.'

'Okay. And, hey—That really is a handsome

162

jacket.'

'I prob'ly got nothin' I really need to ask you and may be wastin' your time. But—'

'Not at all Lieutenant Columbo,' said Bruce Emerson, who had agreed to meet him in the walnut-paneled billiards room and bar of the University Club. 'I think I understand what you have in mind; and if I were you, I'd have that in mind, too.'

'I could be all wrong,' said Columbo. 'Y'see, I'm no genius, Mr. Emerson. I just have to look at the obvious and see if it leads me anyplace.'

'So the agent and business manager for Jonathan is obviously a suspect in the death of Betsy Clendenin.'

Columbo turned up the palms of his hands and turned down the corners of his mouth. 'What would you think if you had the case?'

Emerson smiled wryly. He was a man of maybe forty or forty-five years, heavyset, with curly dark hair retreating off his great head. He wore eyeglasses that rested on the tops of his cheeks. His jacket and slacks were much like Columbo's.

'Seat at the bar? What's yours, Lieutenant?'

'Well, maybe a light Scotch.'

Emerson chuckled. 'A *light* Scotch is J&B. A double for the lieutenant. With a splash of

163

soda? And the same for me. Do you play billiards, Lieutenant Columbo?'

'I play pool, Sir. I play nine-ball, mostly.'

'Good at it?'

'Well . . . reasonably.'

'We'll have to try a game sometime. Myself, I play billiards. You know the game?'

'I know the idea. I never played. There's no billiards tables in the places where I play pool.'

'Lieutenant, when we have time, there's a game I'd like to play with you. Snooker. Have you ever played snooker?'

'As a matter of fact, I have, Sir.'

'Like billiards, snooker is a game of skill. Forgive me, Lieutenant, but nine-ball is a game of luck, largely. But snooker—Billiard-size table. Pockets with round corners instead of angled ones—made to *reject* the ball rather than welcome it in.'

'It's a very tough game, Mr. Emerson. I like it, though.'

'You figure I had something to do with the death of Miss Clendenin,' Emerson said with a sudden change of mood. 'I have fifteen percent of Jonathan. You know how much money that came to. You know about what it comes to now. Well—I didn't kill her. And I don't know who did.'

'That's what I'm tryin' to find out. Who did?'

'I'm going to tell you something in perfect frankness, Lieutenant Columbo. When we learned what Miss Clendenin was doing to Jonathan, we had a meeting; and we actually discussed the question of whether or not we should kill her.'

'Who?' Columbo asked.

'Myself. Marcus Detwiler. Seizo Asano— the president of the recording company. Jonathan himself. A meeting of the corporation, so to speak. And we decided it would be total foolishness to do anything against Miss Clendenin.'

'But you did think about it.'

'Lieutenant . . . do you understand how much money was involved?'

Columbo nodded.

'For myself, let me explain that nothing of the kind ever crossed my mind. I made a lot of money off Jonathan, but I always understood something the others didn't seem to understand—that Jonathan was a fad and couldn't last forever. In fact, the fascination with androgynous types is fading across the landscape. My idea was to make as much as I could while I could.'

'I can understand your owning a piece of Jonathan,' said Columbo. 'You're an agent; that's your business. And the Japanese gentleman; I can understand that. But why did Mr. Detwiler own a share?'

'He wanted to diversify,' Emerson said simply. He picked up the drink the bartender had just put in front of him. 'Understand, we needed investment capital. It cost a lot of money to merchandise Jonathan. You couldn't just put him out on a stage and start him singing. Also, a man had to be most imaginative to see the potential. Marcus Detwiler was actually the key. He put up a lot of money.'

'Did he get it back?'

'You better believe he got it back!' Emerson laughed. 'He owns thirty-five percent.'

Columbo took a swallow of Scotch and soda. 'How come the little girls?' he asked.

Emerson paused, drawing a deep breath, before he said, 'Jonathan's a sad figure, Lieutenant. A sorrowful man. He's childlike in many respects. He likes little girls because they're his devoted fans, also because they don't try to compete with him or to dominate him, as mature women have done. I very much doubt he ever did what Betsy Clendenin suggested in her book. I've never seen him touch one of those girls. He plays with them. They play croquet with him—'

'Naked?'

'As a matter of fact, yes. And even when he runs his electric trains for them. He enjoys seeing them. I really don't believe he ever touches them. Marcus always made quite a point of having their parents present. Of course, he's made more of a point of it since the book came out.'

'Two girls were mentioned by name in the

166

book,' said Columbo. 'Kitty and Penny.'

'Actually,' Emerson interrupted, 'Penny was mentioned only because she was named by Kitty.'

'Shortly before the book came out, Kitty and her mother disappeared,' Columbo said grimly. 'So did Penny and her father.'

'Marcus arranged for Kitty and Bea Lockhart to go to Brazil,' Emerson said calmly, as if it were nothing unusual.

'Why?'

'We knew the book would be a sensation, but we thought Jonathan might survive it. He wouldn't if Kitty were some way encouraged to make more statements, maybe more specific ones—whether what she charged was true or not. Marcus arranged it all. I didn't have anything to do with it.'

' 'Kay. Then what happened to Penny and her father?'

Emerson shook his head. 'I have no idea.'

'Neither do I, Mr. Emerson. Neither do I,' Columbo said as he took another sip of Scotch. 'But we transferred the case file today—from Juvenile to Homicide.'

'Homicide?'

Columbo nodded. 'Homicide.'

26

TUESDAY, JANUARY 12—9:18 A.M.

'Hey, Columbo! Where's your new threads?'

'Y' can't wear a new jacket every day. I mean—'

'So the peacock has returned to the buzzard.'

'Get lost.'

Columbo was at his desk, with a cup of coffee in front of him. He pulled a hard-boiled egg from his raincoat pocket and peeled it on his desk blotter. He poured on a little salt. With the coffee, the egg was his breakfast.

When he finished the egg, he brushed the shell fragments into his trash can, and then he began to punch in a telephone number.

'Yeah. This is Lieutenant Columbo, Los Angeles Police Department, Homicide Squad. I wonder if it would be possible to speak with Mr. Mahaffey, just for a second or two. Won't take long. Okay.'

Mahaffey came on the line. 'Did you get my FedEx package, Lieutenant? What can I do for you?'

'I sure did, and I thank ya. I got one little question, Sir. It seems like Jonathan's partners out here got a copy of Miss Clendenin's book before it was published. How could they do that?'

'How long before?' Mahaffey asked.

'Two or three weeks. I have to guess about it.'

'Shipments of the book would have been in the stores by then. They're not supposed to put them out before pub date, but sometimes they do. Another thing: we mail copies to reviewers well in advance. Somebody who knew a book reviewer or book-review editor could get a copy that way. It's nothing very difficult, Lieutenant.'

'Okay. That's what I wanted to know, and I appreciate your time.'

'Tell you what I'll do. I'll fax you a list of the Los Angeles publications we mailed review copies to. Let me have your fax number.'

'That's very kind of you, Sir. I've got that number right here somewhere.'

After he hung up the phone, Columbo buzzed Martha Zimmer, and she came to his desk a minute or so later.

'There's somethin' we oughta look into, Martha. Maybe you can handle it for me. Or get somebody to. It seems like the Jonathan group got their hands on a copy of the book before it was published. That may not mean anything, but I'd like to know if they did. There could be two ways of gettin' a copy in advance: one, to get a copy from a reviewer, and, two, to buy one out of a store's stockroom before they put the book out on the shelves.

169

Why don't ya check with the book-review editors first? There aren't too awful many. We'll be gettin' a fax from New York: a list of the places where review copies were sent. Also, ya might cheek the bookstores closest to Mr. Detwiler's office and Mr. Emerson's.'

Martha nodded. ' 'Kay.'

'I gotta catch a plane,' said Columbo. 'I'm flyin' over to Vegas to talk to the guys who are lookin' into the death of Harry Lehman. Uh . . . would you mind takin'me to the airport? I hate to leave my car in the airport parking lot.'

2:37 P.M.

Chief of Detectives Bud Murphy was a young man to hold his rank. He was slight of build and had a shiny bald head and beady brown eyes. He was in his shirtsleeves and wore his shoulder holster and service revolver under his left arm.

'I remember it well,' he said to Columbo. 'You came here when you were investigating the death of Paul Drury. Do you remember me?'

'Oh, sure,' said Columbo. 'I remember, one thing, that you were kind enough to drive me to the airport.'

'How long will you be in town, Lieutenant?'

'I got a reservation on a six-o'clock flight back to L.A.'

'That's too bad. We could've had dinner.'

'I wish we could.'

Murphy leaned back in his chair and joined his hands behind his head. 'Harry Lehman,' he said. 'You faxed that you wanted to talk about Harry Lehman.'

Columbo nodded. 'BATF thinks Lehman may have built the bomb that blew up Betsy Clendenin.'

Murphy grinned and shook his head. 'Paul Drury, Regina, and now Betsy Clendenin. You do get the big ones.'

I'd just as soon get little ones,' said Columbo.

'Well—We haven't got a clue as to who killed Harry Lehman. BATF thinks he was building an occasional bomb for a select group of clients. The FBI may have thought so too.'

'FBI?'

'Right. An agent came to see Harry not long before he died. Interesting, too. The FBI denies it sent anyone to visit Harry Lehman.'

Columbo reached in his raincoat pocket, felt a half-smoked cigar there, but decided not to light it. 'If the FBI denies it, what makes you think he did have a visit from them?'

'His son. Harry asked his son to get the agent a special deal on a room at the Piping Rock. Incidentally, we got nothing on the son. Lots of suspicion but nothing we can prove.'

'That's kind of odd, isn't it?' Columbo

asked. 'To try to set up a deal on a room, for an FBI agent? I never heard of a guy being questioned by the FBI offering the agent a deal on a room. I never heard of an agent acceptin', either.'

3:15 P.M.

Columbo had been in The Piping Rock Hotel and Casino before, during the Drury investigation. It was not one of the very biggest, most luxurious hotel-casinos in Las Vegas. It was smaller than the best-known hotels. Its stage did not feature the major stars featured on the stages of hotels like Caesar's Palace or the MGM Grand; nor did it promise the cuisine or the sumptuous appointments of those hotels. It was, on the other hand, a solid, well-maintained, flourishing establishment, busy twenty-four hours a day.

Charles Lehman was assistant manager of the Piping Rock. He looked as if he were forty years old, roughly: a tall, slim man with thick black hair slicked back as if it were controlled by spray—which it probably was. His nose was long and sharp, his chin was strong, his lips were thin and white. He had, overall, a somewhat forbidding, unfriendly appearance.

He made no effort to give the impression that he was pleased to see the two detectives. He did not ask them to sit down. He simply stood in the middle of the casino, his eyes

172

flitting from table to table, glowering at his dealers.

'What now, Murphy?' he asked.

'This is Lieutenant Columbo, Los Angeles Police Department, Homicide Squad.'

Lehman frowned at Columbo. 'You gonna find out who killed my father?'

Columbo turned down the corners of his mouth, lifted his brows, and shrugged. 'Might happen,' he said. 'Stranger things have happened.'

'I'm not interested in strange things, Lieutenant. I'm interested in who killed my father.'

'I'm interested, chiefly, in who killed Miss Betsy Clendenin,' said Columbo, 'and there's a remote possibility it may have been the same guy. A very remote possibility. But not impossible.'

'What's the connection?' asked Lehman.

Columbo turned up the palms of his hands. 'If we can sit down, maybe I'll tell ya.'

Lehman pointed to the door of the bar off the casino. They went in. It was as it had been when Columbo came here during the Drury investigation: dark and cozy. A young singer sat on a stool and sang, wearing only a pair of bikini panties and black, patent-leather shoes. She was backed by an electronic keyboard and an electric guitar.

Like the girl named Mary Lou that Columbo remembered from his last visit here,

173

she sang favorites.

'This is a very pleasant bar,' said Columbo. 'I enjoyed it when I was here before.'

A waitress saw that Charlie Lehman had come in, and she hurried to their table. Everyone ordered Scotch, and Lehman told her to make them doubles and single-malts. Also, she should bring some peanuts.

'I understand your father had a visit from an FBI agent not long before he was killed,' said Columbo.

'That's what he told me,' said Lehman. 'But Murphy tells me the FBI denies it. Anyway, the agent never showed up. Dad said he'd come, but he didn't.'

'Did your father tell you the agent's name?'

'Yes, he did. But I don't remember it.'

Columbo frowned. 'Suppose I was to write down some names. Do you think you could pick out the name of the agent your father mentioned?'

'I might be able to.'

'Okay. Okay . . . Uh, anybody got a pencil? My wife puts a nice new yellow pencil in my pocket every morning, but I swear I think my pockets eat them up. I never can find one.'

Murphy handed Columbo a ballpoint pen and a notepad. Columbo wrote—

STEFANO
MILLIGAN
KLOSS
MCINTYRE
JAMESON
DOUGLAS

Lehman studied the list for a moment, then put the paper down on the table and tapped on one of the names with his finger. 'That's it,' he said. 'Kloss. My father said an FBI agent named Kloss was in town and that I should fix him up with a nice room at a price.'

27

4:21 P.M.

At Xanadu, Jonathan sat in his chaise longue beside the pool. He wore black satin pants, white socks, no shoes; a long-sleeve white shirt; a broad-brimmed champagne-colored Stetson. At this time of day and this season of the year, the sun shone in under his big umbrella, and he dressed to protect himself from the sun. Jonathan sunburned horribly. Six of his nymphs cavorted in the pool, all of them entirely nude. A parent for each sat and watched from the other side of the pool.

Marcus Detwiler and Bruce Emerson also watched the nymphs, although they were talking with each other and with Jonathan.

'I don't like it a bit,' said Emerson, 'but it's the offer we've got—the *only* real offer we've got. And, hey, $850,000 is not peanuts!'

'For two weeks,' Detwiler growled. 'What we used to make in one night.'

Jonathan covered his eyes—already covered by dark sunglasses—with his hands. 'I'm going to have to sell Xanadu!' he complained in his whiny, high-pitched voice.

'We've got worse problems than that,' Detwiler muttered darkly. 'The case file on Penelope Kent has been moved from Juvenile to Homicide.'

'What does that mean?' Jonathan asked anxiously.

'It means,' said Detwiler, 'that instead of the disappearance of the Kents being investigated by poor little girls from Juvenile, it's going to be investigated by shrewd characters like that disheveled eccentric Lieutenant Columbo. They're on our case already. Brad Reverdy called me this afternoon and told me a woman detective had called him and asked if anyone had asked for the paper's review copy of the Clendenin book.'

'Why in the world would they want to know that?' Jonathan shrilled.

Detwiler looked at him scornfully. 'I have to figure it's because the Lockharts left for Brazil and the Kents disappeared before the book was in the stores. They must think those events were too timely, too convenient, to have been coincidences.'

'They'll never find out what happened, though,' Jonathan whispered, shaking his head. 'You promised me they would never find out.'

'No, they won't find out,' said Detwiler.

'This, I am afraid,' said Bruce Emerson, 'depends on the silence of your friend Jason Gimble.'

'Jason,' Detwiler said somberly, 'will be silent.'

'How can you be sure?' asked Emerson.

'Don't ask too many questions.'

'You promised me that everything would be alright,' Jonathan pleaded.

'Let us not forget, my friend, that it has been your taste for little girls that raised this trouble. Nothing that Betsy Clendenin wrote of you did as much damage as her chapter about your weird habits.'

'That was our deal!' Jonathan wept. 'I'd do the thing. I'd play the freak. You'd give me—'

'Never mind,' Detwiler interrupted angrily. 'You got what you wanted. You still do, damnit. But one of the little bitches talked.'

'And one threatened,' Jonathan sobbed. 'Why? She got everything she asked for! Her father got everything he asked for.'

'He did that,' said Detwiler dryly.

'You can't trust anybody,' Jonathan said disconsolately.

'Lieutenant Columbo?'

Speaking to him was a uniformed officer waiting at the gate as he left the plane at LAX. He nodded at her.

'I'm Catherine Gray, Lieutenant. People call me Cathy. Sergeant Zimmer sent me to meet you. One of her children has a cough or something, so she wanted to go home.'

'Well, I'm sorry to hear that. But I'm glad to meet you, Cathy. Been on the job long?'

'About sixteen months.'

His thought was that she was an exceptionally pretty girl. He realized, though, that it was now considered faintly improper to compliment a working young woman on her appearance—or, of course, to think of her as a girl. Well—To hell with all that. 'You're a very pretty girl, Cathy, if ya don't mind my sayin'. It's a pleasure to meet you.'

'Thank you, Lieutenant. I'd heard of you even before I joined the Department, and I've heard a lot more of you since. It's a pleasure to meet you, too.'

'Ya like police work?'

'Very much. I hope to make detective someday.'

Her black-and-white sat at a yellow curb,

178

just under a NO STANDING OR PARKING—
TOW-AWAY ZONE sign. She knew very well
that no one was going to tow away a police car.

She drove. Columbo would have liked to
light a cigar but decided it wasn't the polite
thing to do inside a closed car.

'You want to go back to the garage
downtown, right?' she said.

'Right. Y'see, my car's a French car, and it's
given me a lot of good service. I'd sure hate to
have it stolen or have some wise guy do any
kinda vandalism on it.'

'I can understand. My boyfriend drives a
Jaguar, and he's always afraid somebody will
steal it. I've told him he ought to just drive a
Chevrolet. Then he'd be more comfortable.'

'Y'probably got a good idea there. My wife
drives a Dodge, and she doesn't worry about
anybody stealin' it.'

Cathy laughed. I have a note here from
Sergeant Zimmer,' she said. She handed him
an interoffice memo envelope: one of those
manila envelopes with holes in it and lines for
routing and rerouting it. Columbo took out the
memo and read it—

I spoke with a Mr. Reverdy of the
L.A. News. He says Marcus Detwiler,
who is a friend of his, called him
and asked for a review copy of The
Real Jonathan. Mr. Reverdy had sent
it out to a reviewer and couldn't

179

oblige Detwiler. But notice that Detwiler did try to get an advance copy. He's a resourceful fellow, and we can figure he got one somewhere.

Columbo folded the note and returned it to the envelope. 'So,' he said, 'you think you wanta be a detective?'

'Yes, Sir.'

'Ya makin' collars regularly?'

'Yes, Sir.'

'What kind?'

'Car thefts, concealed weapons, narcotics. Whenever my partner and I pull over a car for a traffic violation, we check it out.'

'That can be dangerous,' Columbo warned.

'It *is* dangerous. I have a neat little white scar on my hip, where a perp's bullet grazed me. I was lucky; it just grazed me.'

'What happened to the guy who shot you?'

Cathy Gray glanced at Columbo. 'He'll never do anything of the kind again.'

'That's interestin'. In all my years on the job, I've never fired my gun.'

'You think I shouldn't have?' she asked defensively.

'I'm not sayin' anything like that. I guess I've just been lucky. To start with, I was lucky to get to be a detective. And I've been awful lucky in my work. I'm no genius, y'see. I've met detectives that are. But I'm not. I just plug

180

away. You might be better. You might have a special talent for this work, like I don't have.'

'You're too modest, Lieutenant,' she said with a broad smile.

'Yeah . . . Who was it said of some guy that he was a modest man with much to be modest about? That's me, too.'

28

WEDNESDAY, JANUARY 13—9:21 A.M.

Wednesday morning Columbo met with Captain Sczciegel in the captain's office.

'I've got to be frank with you, Columbo. You've got a real monkey on your back with this Betsy Clendenin case. Marcus Detwiler was at a cocktail party last evening and sort of casually told the mayor that you are meddling in his business. He was being facetious—but not really. The mayor called me at home last night. He says he doesn't want to interfere, but he also says you've got to be very careful. Detwiler has political clout. You don't dare move against him unless you've got overwhelming evidence.'

'Actually,' said Columbo, 'I'm turning more and more toward Frederick Kloss.'

'That's a hot potato, too. You could really make us look bad if you charged a former agent of the FBI with murder. You've got to have it nailed down tight.'

181

'I figured it that way myself.'

'One more thing. Your question about writing a letter in support of a commutation of sentence for Ai-ling Cooper-Svan. I talked it over with the Chief and the D.A. If you want to do it, go ahead. Apparently her lawyer is going to make an appeal for clemency, and there's a good deal of sympathy for the woman.'

'Once in a while, once in a *very* long while, you regret . . . Y'know?'

'I know. A suggestion, Columbo. If you can, wait until after you get this Clendenin thing cleared up. You don't want to send the letter if you've got egg on your face.'

'Right. Understood.'

Martha Zimmer knew how to get Columbo's attention for a memo or telephone note—wrap it around a cigar and leave it on his desk. He stopped by his desk a little before ten o'clock. Finding Martha's note, he buzzed her on the phone. She wanted him to go to Juvenile with her and meet with Sergeant Margaret Phillips.

'Hiya, Phillips! How's the headache today?'

'So far it's a lucky day.'

'Good. Ya got somethin' for us?'

'Maybe. An idea. You remember I told you, after the Clendenin book on Jonathan came out, we got a warrant and entered the Lockhart apartment and the Kent apartment. Because it looked like the Kents had left abruptly, without packing anything, we rummaged around a good deal. One of the things I looked at was Edward Kent's checkbook. He had a checking account in the United California Bank, Santa Monica branch. He was careless about the checkbook, didn't write down his balance or his checks. It occurred to me that it might be a good idea to see what kind of a balance he had.'

Columbo nodded. 'Good thinkin'. I guess we'd have to get a court order to take a look at that bank account, since the man's not officially dead.'

'It's the kind of thing you can do when you decide you're looking at a homicide,' said Sergeant Phillips. 'The kind of thing you don't have time to do when all you have is a missing juvenile whose parent is also missing. You want to know how many files I have open? This morning, fifty-eight.'

'We got lotsa open files in Homicide, too,' said Columbo. 'Martha's probably got—Anyway. Bank account.'

'You know what we might find?' Sergeant Phillips asked, warming to her subject. 'We just might find that Edward Kent has written checks since he disappeared in August. Wouldn't that be interesting?—to find he's cashed checks in Florida or Texas. Put a whole new complexion on the case. If he's alive somewhere and Penny's with him, that'd close Homicide's file on the case.'

'I figure we gotta get a court order.'

'I already got it,' she said. 'I talked to the Assistant D.A. yesterday.'

'Sergeant, you're a gem!'

'Call me Peg,' she said.

11:30 A.M.

In an office at United California Bank, Columbo and Peg Phillips sat down at a computer terminal, and a young man tapped keys and brought up on the screen the record of the Edward Kent checking account.

'That's a hefty checking account . . .' remarked the young man.

It *was* a hefty checking account. The balance in it was $92,381.34.

'Go back six or eight months,' said Peg.

The young man tapped keys to do that. 'Not so hefty here,' he said.

On May 23 the balance had been $410.19. That was followed the next day by a deposit of $10,000. Another $10,000 was deposited on June 12, followed by another $10,000 on July 3. Then on July 20 Kent had deposited $20,000. On August 18 he had deposited $50,000. In the same period, Kent had written only four checks.

'What's the pattern?' Peg asked Columbo.

Columbo scratched his head and twisted his mouth. 'For a guess, I'd say Mr. Kent was accumulating cash, gettin' ready to lam.'

184

'*What* did he deposit?' Peg asked the young man. 'I mean, if it was checks can you tell whose checks they were?'

The young man shook his head. 'It was cash. See the symbols on the July 20 and August 18 deposits? The bank has to report cash deposits of that size to the federal government—which we did; that's what those symbols mean.'

Columbo pinched his chin. 'No checks written since that one for a couple thousand on August 23. If Mr. Kent's still alive, he's livin' off something besides his money in this bank.'

'If . . . Is that the reason for the inquiry?' the young man asked.

'That's the reason,' said Columbo. 'The man has disappeared. Which is not unusual. But it sure is unusual for a man to disappear and leave that much money untouched.'

12:45 P.M.

'Introducin' ya to somethin' *great*, Peg. You can't get better chili anywhere in Los Angeles. I mean, you did say you like chili. Well, the way Burt makes it—Hey, you can't *get* it any better.'

Sergeant Peg Phillips glanced skeptically around Burt's. The habitués looked up from their bowls of chili and their games of pool, at the attractive blond woman with the police badge. They were accustomed to Columbo coming in here, and he did not make them uneasy. He had a sense of humor, as they saw him; but this somewhat stern-looking woman might not—and some of them had little secrets they would rather have addressed with a sense of humor.

'Play pool?' Columbo asked.

'Never tried,' she said.

'Wasted my youth. My father loved the game, and I guess I inherited that from him. I suppose it's funny that I drive a French car, because I'm Italian, y'know. I'll tell ya somethin' you won't believe. My grandparents made wine. And they let me stomp grapes! Can ya believe it? Down in the cellar, in a big wooden vat. I'd wash my feet and roll up my pants and get in there and stomp. Usually it was my sister that did it. I can see her now: skirt hiked up, stompin' around, mashin' grapes. She didn't like to do it. She thought it was a too—Italian thing to do and didn't want her friends to know about it. It was a chore for her. But not for me. I loved it. I'd do it right now if I could find—Well . . . I'm not *really* nuts.'

Peg laughed. 'The last thing in the world I'd call you is nuts.'

'We'll have two bowls of chili, Burt—with lotsa crackers as usual. And what? Pepsi?'

'Fine,' she said.

'That bank account writes a scenario,' said Columbo. 'You figure Kent started to blackmail

186

the Jonathan organization. The sequence of deposits sure look that way, don't they? Deposits got bigger and bigger. And in cash. The account confirms exactly what you suspected.'

'Some more speculation,' said Peg. 'Kitty and her mother didn't want to testify against Jonathan, if it came to that. What you want to bet that Kent threatened Penny would? He probably got pretty pushy.'

'Yeah. Even so we don't know he and Penny are dead, much less who killed them. I like to crush my crackers into my chili.'

'You're not going to give up on this thing, are you, Columbo?'

He put a spoonful of chili with crushed crackers' in his mouth and chewed. 'Naah,' he said. 'I'm not gonna give up.'

'Well, look who's here! Do I know Columbo or do I know Columbo?'

Adrienne Boswell had come in. She was wearing faded stretch jeans and a UCLA sweatshirt.

'Adrienne . . . Adrienne Boswell, meet Sergeant Peg Phillips of Juvenile Division.'

'No wonder I can't get to first base with this guy,' said Adrienne with a grin. 'Any girl he brings to Burt's—'

'Now, Adrienne, now.'

Peg smiled. 'So. I figured there had to be somebody someplace.'

Adrienne laughed. 'No way! He's as loyal to his wife as he is to that grotesque raincoat.'

PART FIVE

'My father loved to play pool. I inherited that from him. And these cuff links. See? They're little racks of pool balls. They're real gold, my mother said. I never had the heart to let a jeweler look at them. If they're not real gold, I don't want to know it.'

'The man who hands me a film of Marilyn Monroe being fucked by either one of the Kennedy brothers will be set up for life!'

—JOHN EDGAR HOOVER

29

1:32 P.M.

Adrienne sat down beside Peg Phillips and ordered a bowl of chili—'My concession to this friendship.' They chatted about things inconsequential until they had finished their chili, then Adrienne suggested they 'stroke a little pool.' Peg said she had to get back to the office. She was driving, and Adrienne said she would drive Columbo back to headquarters.

She lost the lag, and Columbo broke the rack. He sank the one- and two-balls, then missed the three.

'I spent a couple of hours with Linda Semon,' said Adrienne as she took aim on the red three. 'She let me listen to her tapes.'

'Hear anything interesting?'

'If you're interested in savaging the remnants of Hoover's reputation, yes. If you want to solve the conundrum, no. Or maybe not completely no.'

She missed the three but left it frozen on the top rail. Columbo shook his head and took a shot that barely kissed the ball and sent the cue ball back to the bottom rail. 'Tell me about it.'

'The tape is of an interview with another retired agent, this one by the name of Roger

Fraser. He lives in Bethesda, Maryland. He hated J. Edgar Hoover. I'd like to know what Hoover did to him. It doesn't make him the world's most reliable witness, but frankly that wouldn't have made much difference to Betsy; she'd have used his statement anyway.

'So what'd he say?'

'Fraser must be the source from which Betsy got the idea of the relationship between Director Hoover and Roy Cohn. Linda says there was other evidence of that but it was destroyed in the explosion. Fraser says that Cohn was an overnight guest at the Director's house many times. He gave Hoover a painting by Thomas Hart Benton—about as explicit and erotic a nude as anything ever turned out by a major artist. The painting was found in Hoover's house when his estate was appraised, but no one knew where he got it. Well, according to Fraser he got it from Cohn. It was a gift from Cohn to Hoover.'

'How does he know?'

'He says Hoover sent him to New York in an FBI station wagon to get the picture. It was too big to take on a plane. Cohn traveled back to Washington with Fraser, and on the way Fraser unwrapped the painting, showed him what it was, and told him it was a gift for the Director.'

'Which proves what?' Columbo asked.

'It proves that Roy Cohn gave J. Edgar Hoover a gift that was worth a good many thousands of dollars. Either it was a gift to a lover or it was in payment for favors done.'

'Which does Fraser think it was?'

'He thinks it was a payoff for something Hoover had done for Cohn.'

'Wouldn't it have been simpler to pay him off with money?'

'J. Edgar Hoover had a special fascination with nude pictures and sculptures. His house was full of them. He would have appreciated the painting more than its equivalent in money. Besides . . . a picture by *Thomas Hart Benton!* That was one hell of a gift, Columbo.'

'I guess that three-ball is poison. Neither one of us can sink it, it looks like. Maybe it would be a good idea for Miss Semon to put those tapes away in a safe place.'

'Already done. We had two sets of copies made, then rented a safe-deposit box and put the originals in. Also, except for you and me and Roger Fraser, no one knows the tapes exist.'

'You plannin' on doing anything with them?'

'I'm going up to see Ai-ling Cooper again,' Adrienne said as she took aim on the red ball. 'Hah! There, by damn! Now—Oh god, look at the four-ball!'

'By the way, I'm authorized to write a letter to the D.A., saying I wouldn't oppose a commutation of sentence for Mrs. Cooper.'

'Can I tell her?'

'Why not? Maybe she better have her

lawyer talk to me about it.'

'She'll be grateful. Anyway, I'm going to propose to Ai-ling that Linda and I co-author an article for *Glitz*. Betsy's last article will be running next month. In, say, April or May there'll be *our* article, saying it was what Betsy would have published if she had not been killed.'

Columbo frowned and shook his head. 'That could be dangerous, Adrienne.'

She grinned. 'I'm counting on your having the killer behind bars before the article comes out.'

Columbo grinned. 'You're a pro, Adrienne. I'm glad we're always on the same sides of things.'

'I'm going to drive you back to headquarters. How'd you like to listen to the tape? I've got it in the car.'

She plugged the tape player into the cigarette-lighter socket. They sat outside Burt's and listened to the interview between Betsy Clendenin and Roger Fraser. Fraser quoted Hoover many times. Some of the quotes would stick in Columbo's mind—

'One of those new guys that just graduated from the FBI Academy is a pinhead! Get rid of him!'

Fraser explained that administrators checked the hat sizes of all the new agents and

194

assigned the loser to the Seattle office, where the Director would never see him again.

'It's common knowledge that coons have bigger whangs than white men—which makes them more lubricious. That's what makes them so dangerous to white women.'

'There's no such thing as a Mafia. No such thing as organized crime. All we have in this country is a bunch of petty crooks, some of which know each other.'

'The man who hands me a film of Marilyn Monroe being fucked by either one of the Kennedy brothers will be set up for life!'

'You show me a man that doesn't wear a hat, and I'll show you a man with no respect for himself!'

'We got clods at the SOG! Get rid of them!'

In response to this, Fraser explained, administrators of the FBI formed what they called a 'Clod Squad' to find out who were 'clods' at the Seat of Government.

2:17 P.M.

'I hope I'm not makin' a nuisance of myself, Sir, but I do have a question you can maybe help me with.'

'Come in, Lieutenant Columbo,' said Fritz Kloss. 'Like I said, any time I can do anything

195

for you—'

Columbo entered Kloss's living room and sat down on the couch as Kloss gestured he should do.

'I can't get it outa my mind,' said Columbo, 'that Miss Clendenin was killed while she was working on a book about Director Hoover. The Director's been dead a long time. Who could be hurt today by a book about him, no matter how mean and dishonest it might be?'

'Well, a lot of us thought the Director was a genuine American hero.'

'Sure. Lots of people think General MacArthur was a great American hero, but who'd kill somebody who was writin' a book saying he wasn't? That doesn't make sense, do ya think? Tell me what you think. You got a lot of experience investigatin' crimes.'

'I suppose there are some who would do just about anything to protect the Director's reputation,' Kloss said grimly.

'Yes, Sir. But I can't help thinking it's gotta be something more than that.'

Kloss shrugged. 'God knows.'

'Right. A name did come up. Did you ever hear of an FBI agent by the name of Fraser? Roger Fraser, I think it was.'

'It seems to me I do remember a man by that name. Worked at the Seat of Government . . . Washington.'

'Would he have worked close to the Director? I mean, did he do personal things

196

for him?'

'Lieutenant, all of us who worked at the Seat of Government were sometimes called on to do things for the Director. Sometimes, I'll be frank to say, we had to wonder if they were not personal and maybe didn't actually have anything to do with duty. We had so much confidence in the man, we never questioned. I sometimes did things that looked like personal errands. But I could never be sure the Director wasn't sending me into situations where he expected me to observe. Fraser . . . I hardly remember him. Is he important?'

'Well, he gave Miss Clendenin a personal interview. She mentioned that he said some important things. 'Course, we'll never know what he said to her—won't, that is, unless he decides to talk to somebody else. Whatever he said to her, the record of it was lost in the explosion.'

'A tragedy.'

'Yeah. Well, I'm sorry to be takin' your time. I thought you might know somethin' about this Fraser fellow that could be helpful.'

'I'm sorry if what I know is not helpful, Lieutenant Columbo.'

'I'll be on my way, then.'

'Stop by any time, Lieutenant. I'm an old war horse, you know; and having some part in an investigation, no matter how small, reminds me of old times and sets the juices flowing.'

Columbo stepped out through the door,

into an afternoon when smog had chosen to settle down over Los Angeles. 'Oh,' he said. 'Excuse me. I'd like to ask you one more little thing. I shouldn't bother you with a question like this. Got nothin' to do with the case. I gotta go over to Las Vegas. I wonder if you know a hotel you could recommend—you know, one the old expense account can stand. Fellas that go on official business can't afford those big luxury hotels they got there.'

Fritz grinned and shook his head. 'I've been in Vegas only twice in my life . . . and that was many years ago.'

30

THURSDAY, JANUARY 14—10:18 A.M.

'Mrs. Howard? I hope I'm not disturbing your morning, Ma'am. I'm Lieutenant Columbo, LAPD Homicide. Here's my identification.'

A steely-faced woman stood in the doorway of her apartment and stared unamiably. When she saw his identification and realized he was not a door-to-door salesman, she unbent but only slightly. 'Homicide. . .' she said. She sighed. 'Okay. Whatta ya want?'

'I got a question or two I'd like to ask, if ya don't mind,' said Columbo. 'I don't mean to be a nuisance, but if you'd let me come in I—'

'Alright, come in. That's my living room. Siddown. What has Homicide got to do with me?'

'Nothin'. Just thought you might be able to help me a little bit. It's got to do with Edward Kent and his daughter Penny.'

'I talked to the woman from Juvenile Division, told her all I know about the Kents.'

'We now think they may be dead.'

'*Murdered*, you mean?'

It could be,' said Columbo. 'That's why I'm here: a homicide detective.'

Mrs. Howard ran her hand back over her severely combed gray hair, then used both hands to adjust her gold-rimmed eyeglasses. 'I suppose they were the kind of people that could get murdered.'

'Just about anybody can get murdered, Ma'am, but what ya got in mind?'

'Ed Kent wasn't a very nice man, Lieutenant Columbo. He kept late hours, left his daughter alone in their apartment when she was only ten years old or so, brought home bad women, drank a lot, smoked a lot, and—Besides that, I don't think he ever had a regular job. He didn't keep the schedule of a man with a job. I figured he was a drug dealer or a pimp.'

'What about the daughter?'

'Well, what kind of chance did the poor little thing have to grow up into a decent woman? By the time they vacated here, she was already a slut.'

'Did they have any family, any friends?'

'Not that I ever saw. I told all this to the

199

woman from Juvenile.'

'I read Sergeant Phillips's notes. I'm sorry to ask you to repeat things you already told. I wonder, though, if knowing we think both Kents may have been murdered doesn't put things in a different light. I mean, does it make you remember anything you didn't think was important enough to talk about when you talked to Sergeant Phillips?'

'Well, there was the car.'

'What about a car, Mrs. Howard?'

'Ed Kent didn't have a car. All the time he lived here, he didn't have a car. I figured he couldn't afford it. Then, a couple or three months before he scrammed, a car shows up. A damned expensive car: a Mercedes. He drove it. He'd bring home his girlfriends in it. After he and his daughter . . . disappeared, the car disappeared too. I figured he couldn't make the payments on it, so it was repossessed.'

'He could have made the payments, Ma'am. When he disappeared, he left almost a hundred thousand dollars in a checking account. Tell me about this car. Did it have California plates?'

'Uh . . . Yeah, I guess it did. Of course, I didn't get the number. I mean, why—?'

'What kind of Mercedes was it? What color?'

'A little one. Like a sports car, a convertible. Silver-gray. Pretty new, too, I'd guess.

Pimpmobile, I called it.'

'Okay. Anything else?'

'No, I—' Mrs. Howard stopped abruptly, pulled off her glasses, and used her fingers to wipe tears from her eyes. 'You really think that poor little thing was murdered?'

'That's what I'm tryin' to find out.'

Mrs. Howard followed him out of the apartment building and stood on the stoop. 'Is that your car? You drive a foreign car,too?'

'Yes, Ma'am. My car's a French car. They really know how to make'em over there.'

The woman raised her chin. 'I wouldn't know. My late husband sold American cars. We might have been better off if he'd sold a foreign car instead of Fords.'

'Ford's a good car, Ma'am. It's just that— Oh, say. There is one more little thing I s'ppose I ought to ask. You say Penny Kent was a slut. How you figure that?'

'There were nights she didn't come home. I'm not a busybody, Lieutenant, but there were nights when he came home and she didn't. Now where was she?'

'Where you figure?'

'With the man who delivered her home, sometimes as late as eight in the morning, when she'd be late for school.'

'Y'got any idea who that man was?'

'No idea. He delivered her in a big Mercedes, that one silver-gray, too. He'd just let her out, and she'd let herself in with her

201

own key. Damnit, Lieutenant! Ed Kent was a pimp, and he was selling that girl! God knows to who.'

'You don't know to who?' Columbo asked.

'No. How could I know?'

'You find yourself a copy of a book called *The Real Jonathan* by Miss Betsy Clendenin, and you'll find out who. I thank ya, Mrs. Howard. I hope I haven't taken too much of your morning.'

10:49 A.M.

In a drugstore on Sunset Boulevard, Columbo used a pay telephone—

'Motor Vehicles? Columbo, Homicide. Listen, I need a check on a car and a driver's license. Okay. The guy's name is Edward Kent—that's E-D-W-A-R-D space K-E-N-T. Yeah, I'll wait.'

While he waited he stared at the cigars on the shelf behind the cash register. Yeah. He could buy some cigars here.

This kind of stuff was all computerized today. A check that would have taken days just a few years ago could be done in half a minute today.

'Y' got? Driver's license he had. Showin' what address? Check. What I figured. Car license, no. Uh . . . y' got any violations on him? I'll wait.'

Columbo checked his raincoat pocket. Cigar

202

stub. No whole cigars. Lucky he'd decided to call from this place. He'd buy, say, six. They'd probably give him a pack of matches. Which he'd lose. He never lost cigars, just matches. He wondered why that was.

'Oh? Stop-sign violation. When? July? First-class! If he didn't own a car, whose car was he driving? Gimble . . . Jason Gimble. What ya show for an address for him?'

On the street, unlocking his car, Columbo smiled to himself and thought about how almost impossible it was for a man to move through this life and leave no record of himself.

12:00 NOON

Vista del Mar. Columbo walked up the steps and to the door of an apartment building that had known better times but was still elegant in a seedy way. It had been a fine building in the 'forties, probably also the 'fifties.

The name Jason Gimble was on a mailbox and on the buzzer panel. Columbo buzzed the apartment three times. When he got no response, he buzzed the super.

'Who?'

'Lieutenant Columbo, Homicide Squad, Los Angeles Police.'

He had interrupted the superintendent's lunch, as was obvious from the sandwich the black man brought with him to the door.

203

'Lookin' for Mr. Gimble,' said Columbo.

'Ain't seen him since . . . oh, since last summer. He's aroun' someplace, though. Sends his rent every month. Or so the man who owns the building says. Man says Mr. G. pays his rent on time every month, so don't go in that apartment, don't disturb anything.'

'Y' mean he . . . disappeared?' Columbo asked.

'I guess you could say it that way. One day he jus' wasn't here no more. Surprise. Nice young man. Had a nice car.'

'What kind of car?'

The super grinned. 'Bee-yootiful car! Mercedes-Benz. I bet it cost him fifty thousand if it cost him a nickel.' The man shrugged. 'Then—Gone. Car and man. Cops come lookin' for him one time. But I told 'em he wasn't here, hadn't been here for two or three days—as it was at that time. I figure he'll show up again one of these days.'

1:22 P.M.

'There's what ya call fried clams, right?' Columbo asked with grinning enthusiasm.

'I have to admit, man, you are the gourmet of hot dogs, chili, and fried clams,' said Martha.

'It's in the sauce; it's in the way he makes the sauce. Clams are clams, I s'pose. But . . .'

Three of them sat on a wooden bench

facing the beach at Santa Monica. There should not have been surfers at this time of year; but there were, young men and women in rubber suits, riding the curlers.

The third person was Sergeant Peg Phillips. Since the Kent case had been hers, Columbo thought she should be kept in the loop.

'What would ya call it?' Columbo asked. 'Would you say the case has gone to another dimension? Is that the right word to use?'

'The poop sheet on Jason Gimble puts the case in a new light,' said Peg.

Martha handed Columbo a printout—

Subject: Gimble, Jason (1963 – ?)
Arrested L.A. County, grand larceny, auto, 12/18/91; disposition: sentenced six months, released 05/30/92.
Arrested L.A. County, assault w/deadly weapon, 03/04/93; disposition: sentenced one year, released 04/21/94.
Arrested L.A. County, assault, 07/06/95; disposition: dismissed.
Arrested Fairfield County, CT, assault w/intent to kill, 01/30/96; disposition: sentenced one to three, CT State, released 11/21/97.
Arrested L.A. County, 02/07/98, assault w/deadly weapon; disposition: dismissed.

'A professional thug,' said Martha.
'Gone but not forgotten,' said Columbo.

'How come Edward Kent was driving his car? And where is Mr. Gimble now?'

'People in this case have an odd way of disappearing,' said Peg.

'Who was the arresting officer, last time?' Columbo asked.

3:36 P.M.

'Richard Tracy!' said Columbo. I bet ya get an awful lot of kidding about that.'

Detective Tracy grimaced. 'I've been known to take a shot at the jaw of guys that kidded more than once,' he said.

'Don't blame ya, don't blame ya,' said Columbo.

Tracy had responded to a radio call—unlike Columbo he drove a city-owned car with a radio in it. He was one of the few detectives on the force Columbo did not know, though he remembered seeing him in Parker Center a few times. They sat at the counter and drank Pepsis.

'I'm surprised you don't play pool,' Columbo told him, 'Most guys—'

Tracy interrupted. 'This seems like a decent place,' he said, 'but most places where pool is played are not. I'm a Christian, Lieutenant. I try not to go into places where unsavory activities and attitudes are—'

Columbo interrupted in turn. 'Pool is a very Christian game, Tracy. It's a game of skill. A

206

man has to discipline himself to practice, to learn to play pool the right way. It's not a game for loafers and drunks.'

'I'm glad to hear it,' said Tracy superciliously.

'Well—What I wanted to ask you about is a fella named Gimble, Jason Gimble. He's got quite a rap sheet. You arrested him twice, including the last time he was arrested. You remember him? Know anything about him?'

'I know he's dead,' said Tracy laconically.

'How'd he get dead?'

'Drove his car off the road up in the San Gabriel Mountains.'

'When?'

'I think it was in August.'

'Accident?' Columbo asked.

'So it was said. He was full of booze.'

Columbo's attention was for a moment distracted by a man lining up an exceptionally difficult shot in a game of nine-ball banks. The four-ball, which he needed to sink, lay on the edge of the lower right corner pocket. He stood at the bottom of the table, and the cue ball lay near the spot. He drove the cue ball to the right rail about three quarters of the way up the table, from where it bounced against the top rail, then against the left rail and came down to knock the four-ball into the pocket.

'See what skill that took? I can make a shot like that once in a very long while, but—'

'Gimble was a thug,' said Tracy.

'Wondered if he wasn't.'

'The second time I collared him—pretty close to a year ago—the complaining witness lost his nerve and wouldn't testify against him.'

'What kinda work was he in? Drug dealer?'

Tracy shook his head emphatically. 'He was a legbreaker, an enforcer.'

'For who?'

'Detwiler.'

Columbo frowned hard. Again for a moment he watched the man who could shoot banks make another tough shot. 'Begins to fit together,' he said to Tracy. 'Yeah. It does fit together. I bet I can tell ya what kind of car he was drivin' when he went off the road.'

'Tell me.'

'A silver-gray Mercedes convertible.'

'You got it. What's up, Lieutenant? You making a homicide out of that wreck?'

'It's possible, Tracy. It's very possible.'

'I'll send over the file on Gimble.'

'I'd appreciate that. And one more thing— What would that car he drove be worth? Fifty grand, y' suppose? And could he make enough as a legbreaker to drive a car like that? I've been to his apartment building, and it didn't look like a place that would match a fifty-grand automobile.'

Tracy shrugged. 'It wasn't his. The title was in his name, but it was bought by Detwiler. That's an affectation of his. He's got a fleet of silver-gray Mercedes-Benz automobiles, in various models. But he titles them in the names of guys that work for him.'

'Ah-ha,' said Columbo with a smile spreading over his face. 'That would explain why Gimble would loan his expensive car to Edward Kent. He was deliverin' his daughter to Xanadu in luxury style.'

31

FRIDAY, JANUARY 15—8:38 A.M.

Columbo stood for a moment in thick fog on West Santa Monica Boulevard and looked at the wreckage of Betsy Clendenin's house. A bulldozer with a front loader still stood on the lawn, but most of the debris had been loaded up and hauled away. The other houses had been repaired, though some of the new materials had yet to be painted and looked raw.

He pinched out the little fire remaining in his cigar, deposited it in his raincoat pocket, walked to the house three doors down the street, and pressed the button to ring the bell. Edmund Agon opened the door.

'Good morning, Sir. Do you remember me? Lieutenant Columbo, LAPD Homicide.'

The middle-aged, half-bald Agon was up and dressed, though he had not yet tied his necktie or donned his jacket. He nodded. I remember,' he said without enthusiasm.

'I guess I do have a way of showin' up at inconvenient times, but I wanted to catch ya before you leave for your office. I won't take but a minute of your time.'

'Okay. What can I do for you?'

'Well, you see, we still don't know who killed Miss Clendenin. I got a pretty good idea, but I can't prove anything. There's a way you might be able to help me.'

Agon became more interested. 'Anything I can do,' he said. 'Anything at all, within reason. Uh . . . . come on in.'

'Thank ya, Sir. Your repairs all finished?'

'All finished. A lot of glass, Lieutenant. A lot of glass. Even the glass shower doors were broken. Even so, I'm lucky. Others took much worse damage. Much worse. That was a powerful bomb.'

'Unnecessarily powerful,' said Columbo.

'Let me show you something. Maybe it's what you're here for. Hold on a minute.'

While the man went to get whatever it was he wanted to show him, Columbo glanced around. He supposed the house the bomb had destroyed must have been something like this one: comfortable but not luxurious. Betsy Clendenin had lived well but not ostentatiously.

'Here it is.' Agon shoved some magazines around to protect the coffee table from the sharp edges of the object he put down. 'It's part of a computer. It was on the roof.'

210

The object was a piece of a desktop computer, torn from the rest of the machine and thrown high in the air.

'I don't know a thing about computers,' said Columbo.

'I know just a little,' said Agon. 'What that is is what's called the hard drive or fixed-disk drive. That's part of the computer's memory. Other people around here had so much worse damage to their roofs that I didn't ask the roofers to do anything about mine until the other work was finished. After all, I wasn't getting a leak. Anyway, they went up there and fixed the roof Wednesday. They brought this down, and I said I'd take it for a souvenir. Then my wife said last night over dinner that the thing might be important, might be evidence. If you hadn't come by today I'd have called you.'

'I wonder if it could still have information on it that—I would like to take this thing to headquarters. I'll see that you get it back.'

'I don't really care if I do or don't,' said Agon.

'I appreciate it. Actually, it's not what I came to see you about. Uh, you remember sayin' that your garage door went up mysteriously on the day before the explosion and then on the night of the explosion?'

'That's right. It did.'

'We figure the bomb was detonated by the signal from a radio-controlled garage-door

211

opener. Those things operate on a variety of frequencies, as I understand it. I'd like to check the frequency of yours. My lab people tell me the frequency is printed on the thing somewhere.'

'I'll be happy to have you look at the thing, Lieutenant. Or you can borrow it until your experts figure it out.'

'I thank ya, Sir. It's very kind of you.'

9:21 A.M.

Neither of them could find the frequency number listed on the controller or the opener itself, so Columbo took the controller in his car and drove with it to Las Virgence Road and the home of Fritz Kloss.

Driving by as the sun burned the fog from the air, he stopped across the street and pressed the button.

The retired agent's garage door dutifully rose. One of the two doors to his garage.

Columbo pressed the button again, and the door went down.

9:22 A.M.

Meredith did not have to work this morning, and Fritz had returned to their bedroom and sat propped up beside her, sharing coffee and the morning papers.

They heard the garage door rumble up. In

212

all the years since he had trimmed the antennas the doors had never gone up accidentally. Then, as abruptly, the door rumbled down again.

'What th' hell?'

'Fritz! How can you get excited about—I've read that radio transmissions from airplanes can set them off.'

'Airplane transmissions cannot set them off,' he said grimly. 'Somebody may be playing games.'

'Then change the frequency on the damned thing,' she said. 'Or buy a new one. They're not so much.'

He went to the window and looked out at the street. If someone had set the door going from a car, that car was gone.

10:41 A.M.

When Columbo first called for the services of Geraldo Anselmo, the first computer technician hired by the Department—in the Paul Drury case—Anselmo had been young and a little timid. His technical skills had proved important to LAPD in many cases since then, and he had gained an appropriate measure of self-regard.

'Hiya, Geraldo!'

'Morning, Lieutenant. Understand you're on a big, important case again.'

Anselmo was an American citizen by birth

213

but Mexican by origin. He wore a thin mustache, and he spoke his grammatically flawless and idiomatic English with an Hispanic accent.

'The way I figure, if somebody gets killed the case is as important as any other case,' said Columbo. 'Celebrities' lives aren't any more important than other people's lives.'

'I like your philosophy.'

Columbo laughed. 'Thank ya, Geraldo. Look what I got for ya.'

He had carried the torn and shattered piece of computer to headquarters in a shopping bag Agon's wife had provided. 'There y' are. Careful! The thing's got sharp edges on it. All I want ya to do is revive that computer and make it work again.'

Anselmo grinned widely. 'Next week you shoot a racehorse and haul it in here and ask me to revive it and make it race again.'

Columbo turned down the corners of his mouth and shook his head. 'Can be important,' he said. 'Aren't those brown disks what you call memory? I bet you've guessed what this is, This is a piece of the computer blown up in the explosion that killed Betsy Clendenin. Is there any chance at all, Geraldo, that any of the information that was on those disks survived?'

Geraldo examined the piece of debris. The green circuit board that lay under the disks was cracked two ways. The steel frame of the drive had been twisted when the force of the explosion tore it loose from the chassis of the computer. The disks themselves were warped-deformed by heat or stress or both. Geraldo shook his head.

'Could ya try?'

The technician put the wreckage on his workbench and began to disassemble it with his special tools. He worked patiently and carefully, and shortly he was able to detach the brown disks. Then he partially disassembled an intact drive in another computer and replaced its disks with these. He activated the computer to which the intact drive was attached. The drive grumbled for a moment, then a message appeared on the screen—

ERROR. TOTAL DISK FAILURE, DRIVE C:

Geraldo Anselmo shook his head. 'These things are hardy but not hardy enough to take being blown off the computer,' he said. 'The disks are deformed; that's the problem. The read heads can't read them.'

'No way'round it?'

'One chance in a million. Impossible is a big word, but I'd call recovering data from that hard drive as near to impossible as anything can be.'

Columbo nodded unhappily. 'Geraldo,' he said. 'You're a smart man, know how to make mechanical things work. Is there any chance you make better coffee in this lab than we get

215

anywhere else in the Department?'

Anselmo grinned. 'Espresso?' he asked.

Five minutes later they sat over steaming demitasses of strong black coffee, with twists of lemon peel.

'I don't get this very often,' said Columbo. 'I'm Italian and *should* get it. Remind me to bring you a nice box of amaretto cookies.'

'If the radiation I use to heat the water makes you sterile, don't blame me,' said Geraldo.

'Years ago I'd have worried,' said Columbo.

'Hasn't done it to me.'

'Good. Listen, Geraldo . . . Would you be willing to tell a little white lie in the service of LAPD?'

'What lie would that be, Sir?'

Columbo turned up his palms and smiled slyly. 'Well—Suppose we were to issue a statement sayin' that—miracle of miracles— the information on those two disks survived the explosion. Get me?'

12:47 P.M.

'I see why you suggested I choose a restaurant,' said Adrienne. 'You *wouldn't* take that jacket into Burt's and risk getting pool chalk on it.'

'That's the disadvantage of buyin'expensive clothes,' said Columbo. 'It's *limiting*. Y'know what I mean? Like, could I let Dog shake sand

216

and saltwater on—'

'The raincoat protects it,' she said dryly.

'Well . . .

She had chosen Pacific Vista for their restaurant. She knew Columbo would like the seafood there, and she suggested he try the crabcakes that were the *specialité de la maison*.

'I spent an hour with Ai-ling yesterday,' she said. 'When I told her you would write a letter in favor of executive clemency, it brought tears to her eyes.'

'Aww . . .

'We came to an agreement, she and I. I'm going to pick up Betsy's research as best I can, with Linda Semon's help, and try to reconstruct what Betsy would have said. Ai-ling is going to publish it.'

'That can be dangerous, Adrienne. I got a pretty good idea now who blew Miss Clendenin away, and he's not a man to be messed with. Unless I'm wrong, he murdered somebody else two or three days before he killed Miss Clendenin.'

'Betsy wasn't expecting it. I will be.'

Columbo glanced around the restaurant. He was uneasy about checking his raincoat and wondered if the checkroom girl was taking good care of it.

Actually, that was not what was bothering him. What troubled him was what he pondered saying next. Well—He'd let Adrienne think about it, and decide.

'Adrienne . . . Would you be willing to be bait in a trap?'

She grinned, and he was immediately sorry he had said it. She was so beautiful! She'd come to this meeting in one of the emerald-green outfits that suited her so well, with one of the mini-skirts that also suited her beautifully.

'Forget I said it.'

'No way. What you got in mind, Columbo?'

'In an odd, accidental way we recovered a piece of Miss Clendenin's computer. It was on a roof, three doors down the street, and wasn't taken down till the roofer went up to replace the shingles it had damaged when it fell out of the sky, as ya might say. It's what they call the . . . hard-disk drive, I think is what it's called. Mrs. C studied computers at the university. I'm gonna ask her tonight how a hard-disk drive works. Anyway—'

'Are you going to tell me her data survived?' Adrienne asked excitedly.

'No, that's what I'm not gonna tell you. What I am gonna tell you is, that's what we might say to the world. I had pictures taken of the thing that came down on the man's roof. I'm thinkin' of holding a press conference and saying we're in the process of reconstructing the information that was on that pair of disks.'

'And I could say I'm the intellectual heir to Betsy's work and am going to publish what she had saved on that disk drive!'

'Dangerous . . .'

'And the murderer will come out of the woodwork to try to stop it! Brilliant, Columbo!'

'We'll need Linda Semon's cooperation, also cooperation from Mr. Mahaffey and Mrs. Cooper.'

'I'll talk to Ai-ling and Linda.'

'Alright. I'll call Mr. Mahaffey.'

2:18 P.M.

Columbo sat in Captain Sczciegel's office.

'It won't be the truth, y' understand,' he said to the captain. 'But Mr. Frederick Kloss blew up Miss Betsy Clendenin, and this will smoke him out, I figure. If I'm wrong, it may smoke out somebody else.'

'We'll play it your way, Columbo. You'll have to set up your scenario very carefully.'

'Yes, Sir. I'd like pictures taken of that hunk of computer. We'll hand pictures out to the news people. And I think Geraldo ought to be the one to issue the statement. Not me, anyway.'

'It'll probably come from the Chief,' said the captain.

'Good. That's better yet.'

Captain Sczciegel swung around in his chair and lifted his feet onto his desk. 'If you're so sure of this, why did you ask for the warrant to search the Gimble apartment?'

219

'That's somethin' else. Gimble worked for Detwiler. And there's something very strange. Gimble has been dead for five months, but somebody's still payin' rent for that apartment.'

'The warrant says you want to look for possessions of Edward or Penelope Kent.'

Columbo smiled slyly. 'Or whatever else we might find. But I'm very much interested in finding out what became of the Kents.'

'Take another officer with you,' said Captain Sczciegel. 'I want two witnesses to whatever you find. And call for Forensics if you find anything interesting.'

'I've asked Martha to come with me.'

'Let her drive. She's got a radio in her car.'

32

FRIDAY, JANUARY 15—2:44 P.M.

Marcus Detwiler stood at his office window, with his back to the man in his office. He was looking at rain, which had begun to fall heavily, drifting in sheets on the wind. As always, he was wearing black: suit, shoes, necktie.

'Am I the *only* man in this organization that uses his brains?' he muttered, speaking to himself more than to the other man. 'That goddamned apartment should have been cleaned up within *days* after—*Days*, damnit!'

'I didn't figure it was smart to go near the place,' said the man sitting on the couch. 'The cops might have been watching it. That's why—'

'*For five friggin' months?* And why'd you keep up the rent for all that time?'

'It was our place. We let Gimble live in it for a while, but it's been our place for years. We've kept other guys there. Hey! Remember that broad Fanny? We kept her there for two months while she healed up. We've done a lot of business in that apartment. So I kept up the rent and kept the place available to us.'

Detwiler turned and glared at the man. 'You never told me. Am I not supposed to be smart enough to be told what's going on?'

'Little details, Marcus, little details . . .'

'Oh? How big a detail is it now, Tom? It's only by *luck*, by goddamned *luck*, that I got the word about the search warrant. It's only by luck that the judge's secretary recognized the significance of a warrant to search for possessions of Edward and Penelope Kent. It's only because she's a damned good woman that she gave me a call.'

'What's that woman cost you, Marcus?' the man asked with a leer. 'I guess she's worth whatever it is. How many times has she—?'

Detwiler ignored that and interrupted. 'Okay, tell me, Tom—what's this idiot Columbo going to find if he takes a team into that apartment and conducts a thorough

221

search?'

'I was only in the place one time,' said Tom. His name was Thomas Durant, and he would have been a handsome man except that his nose had been broken to one side and never correctly repaired, so that it was grotesquely twisted. 'I didn't have time to clean up the place. I had to get Gimble drunk and then get him out of there fast, before daylight came. Anyway, I didn't figure that policin' that apartment was my responsibility.'

'What's Columbo gonna find, Tom?'

Durant shrugged. 'Gimble was an idiot, but not in all ways an idiot. He was proud of the job he'd done and told me just how he did it. He knocked Ed Kent and the girl out with chloral hydrate, then strangled them. So this Columbo character is not gonna find blood. He's not gonna find anything that belonged to that pair. They hadn't brought anything. They thought they were there to get another big payoff. Gimble had told Ed Kent he ought to make the girl do somethin' for *him*—I mean for Gimble—in return for that kinda money, which is why they had to meet him at his place. Nobody's gonna find the chloral hydrate. I took that with me when I left the place.'

'Goddamnit, Tom! What *are* the cops gonna find?'

'The only possibility is fingerprints. Maybe the little girl had to go potty while she was there, so her prints might be on something in

222

the bathroom. The little girl drank some Pepsi; that's how Gimble got the knockout drops into her. And Ed drank some Scotch. There might be drinking glasses in the kitchen with fingerprints we wouldn't want the cops to find.'

'*Right!*' Detwiler ejaculated furiously. 'Right! Those goddamned fingerprints could—' He paused and recovered a measure of calm. 'How long would it take you to wipe off the bathroom surfaces and all the bottles and glasses?'

'*Me?*'

'You. I want it done right. More than that, I don't want any more guys to know about any part of this.'

'How many guys know now?' asked Durant.

'You and I. Emerson and Jonathan suspect but don't know. I want to keep it that way.'

Tom Durant smiled. His smile was as twisted as his nose. 'Since it's just the two of us, why don't you come with me? Two of us can work faster than one.'

'Why not? Because that's *your* part of the operation. Anyway, it's the part you screwed up. You go take care of it. I'll give you a hundred thousand as a bonus for taking care of it.'

'How much time you figure I've got?'

Detwiler grinned. 'The judge's secretary held up the warrant as long as she could. The cops didn't get it until an hour ago. You can get over to the apartment and take care of

223

things before they get their act together.'

'Maybe we should've asked Peggy Phillips to come with us,' Columbo said to Martha as she pulled the unmarked car to the curb in front of the building where Jason Gimble had lived. 'After all, it was her case originally.'

'With fifty-something open files on her desk, I don't think she has time to help two of us do a job it only takes two people to do.'

Martha picked up the microphone and reported to the dispatcher. The two detectives were leaving Unit 468 to execute a search warrant. They hurried in, through pelting rain.

Inside the building, Columbo knocked on the superintendent's door. When the man opened the door, he was eating a sandwich as he'd been doing when Columbo interviewed him yesterday.

'Hiya. Back again. This is Detective Sergeant Zimmer. We got a warrant to search that apartment. Wanna let us in?'

The super shrugged. 'Give y' a key,' he said. He stepped back inside his room and pulled a key down from a board. 'That'll let you in.'

'Okay. Thanks. We'll bring it back when we're finished.'

'You don't figure you're gonna find Mr. Gimble *dead* up there, do you?'

'Oh, no. Mr. Gimble is dead alright, but not

224

in the apartment.'

'He's dead? You didn't tell me that yesterday.'

'I didn't know it when I talked to you yesterday.'

'Seems like a shame.'

'Right,' said Columbo. 'He was probably murdered, too. You think about anything else you might remember about him. We might want to talk to you later.'

Columbo mounted the stairs to the second floor. Martha followed.

'Probably a wild-goose chase,' he said. 'Half the work we do, Martha—chasin' after things that don't amount to anything.'

The old building smelled strongly of the oil the super used on its wood floors, which combined with underlying scents of dust and mold to make a heavy, oppressive odor evocative of age and decay—in a building not so old but long neglected. Columbo stared at the key, then at the keyhole, and inserted and turned the key. He gave the door a push and stepped into the living room of the apartment-where the odor from outside was augmented by the vague but definite stench of vacancy.

'Uh . . . Hey! Who are you, Sir? I'm Lieutenant Columbo, LAPD Homicide. I—'

Tom Durant responded by jerking a 9mm Smith & Wesson automatic from under his jacket and firing a single shot at Columbo.

Columbo spun under the impact and

dropped to his knees.

Durant—as if he hadn't noticed Martha—leveled his automatic for a second shot. Martha's slug, from her Beretta, caught him in the belly. He dropped his gun and bent double, shrieking in agony. She stepped forward and brought the weight of her Beretta down on his skull with all her force.

She bolted down the stairs as fast as she could, knocking the superintendent aside. Reaching the car she grabbed up the microphone and yelled into it—

'Unit 468! Unit 468 is still at Vista del Mar location. Officer down! Officer down! Respond with all possible assistance!'

PART SIX

'What ya tryin' to do, kill me with kindness?'

33

4:01 P.M.

The call that an officer was down galvanized the Los Angeles Police Department. Within seconds the dispatcher had backup units and an emergency squad speeding toward the address where Unit 468 had gone to execute a search warrant.

Within a minute the dispatcher reached Captain Sczciegel to report that one of his units was calling 'officer down.' Told that a woman's voice had made the call, the captain realized that the officer down had to be Columbo. He sent a notification team—a chaplain, a paramedic, and an officer from the Detective's Benevolent Association—to tell Mrs. Columbo. It was urgent that the news should come to her from this team and not from the media. Even so, Captain Sczciegel told the team not to go to the door until he advised by radio how bad the situation was.

He commandeered a black-and-white and set off for the Vista del Mar address with siren screaming and lights flashing.

4:02 P.M.

The first backup that arrived was a young officer. He entered the apartment with drawn gun.

He found Columbo lying on his back on the floor, with his head in Martha's lap, conscious and talking quietly. His raincoat lay on the floor near him. Under his left shoulder a gleaming wet bloodstain was already as big as his hand and was still slowly spreading.

Another man lay on the floor, unconscious. A broad stream of his blood ran along the floor.

Using his portable radio, the officer called for a second medical team.

Columbo looked up at the young officer. 'Pick up my raincoat there, will ya? I wouldn't want that blood to get on it.'

4:43 P.M.

When Captain Sczciegel ran up the stairs and came into the Logan Street apartment, the paramedics had Columbo lying on a gurney. They had cut off his jacket and shirt and packed the bullet wound to stop the bleeding. The slug, they said, had apparently glanced off a rib, torn away flesh in his armpit, and ripped through his upper left arm.

The captain squatted beside Columbo. 'I've

230

sent a team to see Mrs. Columbo. They won't go in till I call and tell them how serious it is. I guess I can say you're going to make it, you tough old buzzard.'

'I'm not tough, Captain. I'm just lucky. Isn't it funny? In all my years I've never fired my gun except at the range, and nobody ever took a shot at me. Now . . . The man who does has bad aim. I'm just lucky.'

'Who is he? Do you know?'

Columbo shook his head.

A uniformed sergeant had overheard the question. 'Sir,' he said to the captain, 'here's the man's ID.'

Durant lay on another gurney. The second medical team was working urgently over him. They had cut off all his clothes to get at his belly wound, so he lay naked. He was being dripped with some fluid, through an IV in his arm.

Captain Sczciegel looked at his photo driver's license. 'Thomas C. Durant. Mean anything?'

Columbo shook his head. So did Martha.

'Here's his business card, Sir,' said the uniformed sergeant.

DETWILER SECURITY SERVICES, INC.

THOMAS C. DURANT

Vice-President

A paramedic spoke. 'We'd like to move the lieutenant to the hospital now, Sir.'

'You want to go with him, Martha?' the captain asked.

She nodded. Martha was tearful.

'You better stay here and supervise what's gotta be done, Martha,' said Columbo. 'Get a Crime Scene Unit in here. This Durant fella was no casual burglar. Vice-president of Detwiler Security. He was here for a reason,'

'I'll send word to Mrs. Columbo now,' said Captain Sczciegel. 'I'll go pick her up and bring her to the hospital myself.'

'That's thoughtful of ya, Captain,' said Columbo.

4:44 P.M.

When Martha called for a Crime Scene Unit she specifically asked for Jean Pavlov if she were available. She was, and now she was one of three technicians working in the apartment. As she had when she worked in the Clendenin house, Jean Pavlov wore blue jeans and a gray sweatshirt, with her badge pinned to the sweatshirt.

'What are we looking for, Martha?' she asked.

'This apartment has been vacant for five months or so. The man who lived here died about that long ago, maybe murdered. Even

232

so, the rent has been paid all that time. The man had a criminal record, so we have his fingerprints on file. We'd like to know who besides him was in the apartment. There's an off chance that a missing teenage girl was here. Also that her father was here. We've got his prints, too. I'll have a file put on your desk in the morning, so you'll have all the info.'

'Lotta blood around,' said Pavlov.

'This over here belongs to Lieutenant Columbo. That over there belongs to the man who shot him.'

Pavlov glanced around. 'Well,' she said hesitantly, skeptically, 'we'll do what we can.'

Martha picked up the raincoat from the chair where the young officer had put it.

'That Columbo's?' Pavlov asked.

Martha nodded. 'Yeah. . .' She shook her head. 'That guy! Here he was, shot, and the first thing he did was snatch off his raincoat so it wouldn't get bloody.'

'That thing's ready for the rag bin.'

'No way! Columbo loves it. His new jacket was ruined, but he saved his old raincoat. Look, it's got a bullet hole in it. I'm gonna take it home and darn up that hole.'

34

SATURDAY, JANUARY 16—8:21 A.M.

Captain Sczciegel sat in a chair beside Columbo's bed. Columbo was sitting up and had been trying to unfold and read a newspaper without using his left arm. He was front-page on every paper in town.

'Looks like I can't get rid of you,' said the captain.

'Naah. Not that easy.'

Columbo's left arm was in a sling, and he looked a little pale. Apart from that he seemed little worse for wear. He wore a white hospital gown. Six vases of flowers had already arrived, and an orderly had brought in an extra table for them.

Captain Sczciegel shook his head. 'If you'd been carrying your sidearm, it might have stopped that slug,' he said with a wry smile.

'Yeah. And takin' a shock like that might have set off the bullets in it, and I'd have had an explosion.'

'You're impossible, Columbo. Who'll I turn your cases over to? Ted Jackson? Martha Zimmer?'

'Whatta ya mean, turn over my cases? I'll be outa here Monday.'

'Right. To go home and rest. You can't come back on duty for at least a week, maybe two weeks.'

'What ya tryin' to do, kill me with kindness? I couldn't sit around the house for a week, wonderin' what somebody else is doing with—'

'Columbo—'

'Seriously, Cap'n. I can handle it. I was entitled to tomorrow off anyway. Listen, I appreciate the way you drove Mrs. C here, also the way you talked to her. A policeman's wife always worries about stuff like this. She has to. When we were first married, and I was a cop on the beat in New York, she was just sure somebody'd shoot me. And it never happened. A couple of guys tossed brickbats at me, and bottles. Hit me two times. But—'

'You can't drive.'

'There's people can. In fact, I got one in mind. An officer named Catherine Gray. She'd like to make detective someday, so she can drive me next week and learn a little about detectivin'.'

'Martha could—'

'Martha's got more important stuff to do. She's too valuable to be made a chauffeur.'

'She's a damned good shot with her sidearm, too,' said Captain Sczciegel. 'Fortunately for you.'

'She dropped Durant, for sure.'

'You'll be interested to know that he's going to live. He's got a skull fracture and a punctured intestine, but he's going to survive to face a court on a charge of attempted murder.'

'I got a few questions I wanta ask him.'

'I bet you do. We've got a rap sheet on him. Two arrests for assault and battery, one for assault and battery with a deadly weapon. He did three years in San Quentin for that one. That's where he got his nose busted, if you noticed that.'

'When was this?' Columbo asked.

'It was in 1975, '76, and '77.'

'I bet Mr. Detwiler is feelin' pretty uncomfortable about now.'

9:34 A.M.

So did Bruce Emerson.

'Your vice-president!' he snapped at Detwiler. *'Columbo*, for god's sake!'

They were in Detwiler's office. Detwiler stood staring out the window, with his hands clasped behind his back. Even on a Saturday morning he wore a black suit. Emerson, in a green golf shirt and tan slacks, poured brandy into a snifter, took a big sip, then a sip of coffee.

'Tom Durant has been a valuable man,' said Detwiler without turning.

'I want the truth, Marcus. What was he doing in an apartment that Jason Gimble used to live in?'

Detwiler glanced over his shoulder at Emerson but remained staring down at the street, where yesterday's rain still fell. The streets were almost curb-full of water. 'Are you sure you want to know the truth?' he asked calmly.

'If I'm facing something, I've got to know what I'm facing.'

'*You* aren't necessarily facing anything. You can plead ignorance.'

'Gimble killed the Kents,' said Emerson glumly. 'I'm an accessory to that, and so is Jonathan, if only because we knew it and didn't report it.'

'You *didn't* know it. You surmised it.'

'And you told me not to worry about Gimble talking. "Don't ask too many questions," is what you said. So, Gimble's dead, too, isn't he?'

'We had to cut the number of people who knew down to the one man we could trust for sure,' said Detwiler.

'So we've got three murders to answer for, and now the shooting of a cop. And it all rests on Durant's keeping his mouth shut. Do you trust him that far?'

Detwiler turned away from the window at last and sat down behind his desk. 'I trust him.'

'The guy who pulled a gun and shot a cop? And not just any cop but Lieutenant Columbo! You trust him? He's gonna be facing—What? How many years in the slammer? You think he won't talk to get a reduced sentence?'

Adrienne bent over Columbo and kissed him fervidly. 'Oh, god, Columbo! When I heard the news yesterday evening I all but fainted. Dan thought I was going to.'

'Nothin',' said Columbo. 'Just one of those things that happens. Goes with the work.'

'C'mon. Don't play casual with me. It isn't "nothin'." It's *somethin'*. It's a *big* somethin'.'

'Ya look great, Adrienne.'

She did. She was wearing a white knit mini-dress. She had brushed out her red hair, so that it lay smoothly on her shoulders.

'The nurses say I get no visitors but women. You. Martha. Mrs. C. 'Course, Captain Sczciegel was here.'

'Mrs. Columbo will be here shortly,' said Adrienne. 'I went to your house to see her this morning, after the word was out that you were in no danger.'

'Well, have a seat. I'll be goin' back to work Monday or Tuesday. We're gonna spring that trap. This here sprung one on Detwiler, and I plan on springin' the one we planned on Kloss.'

'Everything's ready, I guess.'

He nodded. 'The Department's holding back the announcement about the computer disk till I'm on my feet.'

'Mrs. Columbo said you'd never hold still

238

for taking a week or ten days off.'

'If there was a reason—'

'Damnit, Columbo, there *is* a reason! You almost got killed.'

'Naah. The only thing that might kill me is boredom.'

2:22 P.M.

Fritz Kloss sat in his easy chair and read another newspaper account of the shooting of Lieutenant Columbo. Meredith, sitting on the couch in her scanties, was watching television; but neither she nor the television distracted him.

VETERAN POLICE DETECTIVE SHOT DOCTORS SAY LIEUTENANT COLUMBO WILL RECOVER FULLY

A veteran Los Angeles homicide detective was shot and gravely wounded yesterday afternoon as he and another detective from the Homicide Squad were executing a search warrant. The doctors who are attending him at the Good Samaritan Hospital say Lieutenant Columbo will recover from his wounds and can return to active duty.

A suspect has been arrested. He is Thomas C. Durant, who was himself shot and seriously wounded by Detective

239

Sergeant Martha Zimmer. Durant is identified as a vice-president of Detwiler Security Services, Inc. Durant was placed under arrest as soon as he regained consciousness in the emergency room at the same hospital.

The police department has issued no statement as to why the two detectives were executing a search warrant at a Vista del Mar address or why Durant was there and shot Lieutenant Columbo.

'What's so interesting?' Meredith asked.

'Oh, nothing special. I'm reading about how this detective named Columbo got shot. I'm not surprised, really. The man is a sloppy, undisciplined oaf.'

She turned her attention again to her television show.

So. Columbo. That nuisance. Fritz guessed he'd seen the last of him.

35

MONDAY, JANUARY 18—2:11 P.M.

With Officer Catherine Gray firmly holding his right arm, Columbo walked into the Homicide Squad office in Parker Center. A little sweat gleamed on his forehead, and he quietly admitted to Cathy Gray that maybe he should have rested this afternoon and come in tomorrow morning.

Wherever he walked in police headquarters, people saluted him. Some applauded.

'Since when does getting shot make a man a hero?' he muttered to Cathy.

He sat down at his desk and began to toss memoranda and report forms into the trash can, glancing for no more than an instant at each one—as Cathy watched in amazement.

Martha appeared. 'Jean Pavlov's got information for you,' said. 'She can come here, or—'

Captain Sczciegel came to Columbo's desk at that moment. 'Use the conference room,' he said. 'Make it the Columbo room for a while.'

Ten minutes later, Jean Pavlov joined Columbo, Martha, Peg Phillips, and the captain in the conference room. Cathy Gray sat down in a chair away from the table, but Columbo waved her forward and told her to sit with the rest of them. 'As long as she has to waste her time hangin' around with me, she might as well get some detectivin' lessons, right?' he said to Sczciegel.

'We hit something of a jackpot in the Vista del Mar apartment,' said Jean Pavlov. 'The variety of fingerprints has got to be interesting. First, there were the prints of Jason Gimble, all over the place. Then, Thomas Durant had touched a bottle and a glass—probably meaning to wipe them off before he left. He'd helped himself to a drink of Scotch. That same bottle also had Gimble's prints on it, and Edward Kent's. And guess what? A glass in the kitchen had on it the fingerprints of Penelope Kent.'

'How'd we come to have a set of prints for her?' asked Captain Sczciegel.

'Standard procedure,' said Peggy Phillips. 'We had a missing juvenile, so we seized a couple of her personal possessions and lifted prints off them, to have her prints on file in case we ever got a chance to identify her.'

'The vacuum picked up three long strands of sandy-red hair,' said Jean Pavlov. 'Female.'

'We took her hairbrush, too,' said Peg Phillips. 'If you want to do a DNA match, we've got the sample.'

Columbo turned to Cathy and said, 'Wouldn't ya hate to be a criminal in this day and age?'

4:47 P.M.

Thomas Durant lay on his back, with an IV dripping fluid through a needle and into his arm. In spite of the fact that he was conspicuously weak and in pain, his right ankle was shackled to the bed.

Captain Sczciegel stood near the bed. 'You don't have to talk with us, you understand. You've been read your rights. You know you don't have to talk to us and that if you do we'll use what you say as evidence.'

'You got all the evidence you need,' said Durant weakly.

'So it won't make much difference, will it? You want to talk? It could be helpful to you. I can't promise anything.'

Durant looked past Sczciegel. 'Who's the crowd?'

Cathy Gray had drawn up a chair for Columbo. 'That's Lieutenant Columbo,' said the captain. 'He's the officer you shot.'

'Sorry about that, Lieutenant. You caught me by surprise.'

'And this is Detective Sergeant Zimmer. She's the one who shot you.'

Durant's eyes narrowed as he focused on Martha. 'I'll hate you for the rest of my life,' he said hoarsely. 'You coulda killed me, and you didn't.'

'I tried,' said Martha dryly.

'And this is Officer Gray. She's got the video camera and will record what you say if you choose to give us a statement.'

'Switch it on, girlie. I'll sing.'

'Sir,' said Cathy to Sczciegel. 'I suggest we read him his rights again, on the tape. From what I understand, he may not have been entirely conscious when he heard them the first time.'

'You've got the card, I suppose,' said Sczciegel.

'Yes, Sir.' She switched on the 8mm video camera; and, holding it in her right hand, she

243

read from the laminated card she held in her left—'

'You are under arrest. You have a right to remain silent. If you choose to make a statement, everything you say will be taken down and may be used in evidence against you. You have a right to the assistance of an attorney. If you cannot afford an attorney, one will be appointed for you at public expense. Do you understand your rights?'

'I've heard 'em before, believe it or not. Could you believe it, that a nice guy like me's been arrested before?'

'Please state your full name and your address for the record—'

Captain Sczciegel asked the first few questions, establishing that Durant was vice-president of Detwiler Security Services, establishing that he had a criminal record, and so on.

'Columbo? Any questions?'

'Well . . . Maybe one or two. Uh. Mr. Durant, how did you get into that apartment?'

'I had a key.'

'How come you had a key?'

'Well, the man who lived there, Jason Gimble, was a friend; and he gave me a key.'

'When did you last see Mr. Gimble?'

Durant frowned. 'I'm not sure. Last week. Tuesday maybe. Maybe Monday.'

'See him often?'

'If you call once every two or three weeks

244

often.'

'So you saw him Monday or Tuesday—or maybe it was Wednesday—and maybe two or three weeks before that.'

'Like that. I saw him just before Christmas.'

Columbo felt a twinge in his wounded arm and faltered for a moment. Martha hurried to him and touched his forehead with a handkerchief. 'You—You a psychic, Mr. Durant?' he grunted.

'Wha'ya mean?' Durant asked, a sudden urgency in his voice.

'Well, ya see, Sir,' Columbo said, stiffening and regaining strength of voice, 'Mr. Gimble has been dead since August of last year. Seems like he got drunk and drove his car off a curve in the San Gabriel Mountains—or somethin' like that.'

'Can't be the same man.'

'Might not, except for a couple of things. The fingerprints on the man found in the wreckage of a Mercedes-Benz automobile matched the fingerprints taken off Mr. Gimble after his many arrests on a variety of charges. What's more, those same fingerprints were found all over that apartment in Vista del Mar. So Mr. Gimble had lived there, but he hadn't been living there for some time. Which brings me back to my first question—what were you doin' in that apartment?'

Durant closed his eyes. 'I'm in pain,' he whispered. He opened his eyes and looked at

245

Martha. 'You shot me in the *gut*. Why not in the heart? Why not in the head? I'm all busted up inside. I may never be able to eat solid food again.'

'Tough,' said Martha. 'Look at Columbo. Four inches to the right, he'd be dead.'

Columbo covered his eyes with his hand. 'Let's don't talk about that, Martha, please. Uh . . . The Crime Scene Unit found somethin' else, Mr. Durant. Two more sets of fingerprints. Do I hafta tell ya whose they are?'

Durant sobbed, and beads of sweat came out on his face. 'What do you guys want from me?' he wept.

'What do you want from us?' Captain Sczciegel asked coldly.

'Put me where they can't get me! Looka my face! That's just a little of what they'll do. Put me in a tough joint, but put me separate from all the guys that want to get me! You got no idea what they're capable of! Put me—Put me where they can't get at me, and I'll tell you everything.'

7:11 P.M.

When two units arrived to serve the arrest warrant on Marcus Detwiler, two other units were already on the street outside his office, together with a medical squadwagon. They had come in response to a 911 call from a cleaning woman employed to clean the offices

246

of Detwiler Enterprises, Incorporated. She had opened his office and found Marcus Detwiler sprawled on the floor behind his desk, dead of a gunshot wound. He had put a 9mm Beretta in his mouth and pulled the trigger.

Bruce Emerson submitted quietly to arrest. He had been waiting for it and had fortified himself with brandy. Officers said they were not sure if he knew where he was going or why.

Deputies who arrived to arrest Jonathan found him cowering behind some shrubbery beside his pool, stark naked and shivering. A naked thirteen-year-old girl held him in her arms and wept.

8:11 P.M.

Adrienne Boswell and Cathy Gray sat with Columbo in his living room—Adrienne in jeans and a sweatshirt, Cathy in her uniform, though she had laid aside the belt that hung her pistol and handcuffs. He had insisted Mrs. Columbo should go on to the university this Monday evening. If she didn't, she would miss the final examination in the course she had been taking in paleontology. She had promised she would come home laden with pizza for them all, but he had told her to concentrate on her examination; he and his two 'girlfriends' would order in their own pizza. In fact, they ordered Chinese. They had cans of beer. Mrs.

247

Columbo had offered glasses, but they drank from cans.

Cathy, who had taken a course in paramedical procedures as part of her work at the Police Academy, changed the dressing on his wound. It was no longer oozing blood and was mostly black scabs. 'Ugly thing, ain't it?' he said.

'It's the most beautiful thing I've ever seen,' said Cathy.

'How ya mean?'

'You're *alive*, Columbo!' She had already picked up the habit of calling him Columbo, dropping the 'Lieutenant' or 'Lieutenant Columbo' she had been using. 'You're alive. It didn't kill you, and that makes it beautiful.'

'Yeah. I guess there's somethin' to be said for bein' alive. I sure wouldn't want to die before I see who wins the Super Bowl.'

'You're a piece of work, Columbo,' said Adrienne. 'You brought down a powerful man. A hell of a piece of what you seem to call detectivin'.'

'Not so good.'

'What do you mean by that?'

'We haven't got the man that killed Betsy Clendenin. That's the point of this month's detectivin'.'

36

TUESDAY, JANUARY 19—9:11 A.M.

Columbo reached into his raincoat pocket for a cigar but once again decided it would be unkind to Cathy Gray to smoke in a closed car.

'Y'know,' he said, 'Martha darning that little hole in my raincoat was one of the nicest things anybody ever did for me. Y'can hardly see it, can ya?'

Cathy shook her head. 'Hardly see it,' she said.

'Well . . . Lotta people want me to retire this raincoat. Like Mrs. C. She thinks I should get a handsome new one. But this coat has a lotta miles on it and a lotta good miles left. I don't believe in giving up on things that still give good service.'

'If it ain't broke, don't fix it,' said Cathy.

'Right. Now, for you it's different. As a uniformed officer, you wanta make a good appearance. And you do. I bet when you stand inspection you get one hundred percent good marks. Your uniform fits. You got all your equipment like it's supposed to be. I mean, you look like a *police officer*.'

'Thank you, Columbo. I try.'

'Glad the rain's stopped,' he said. 'Mud slides got started, y' know. L.A.'s a funny place to live, isn't it? Y' go from drought t' flood.'

'To earthquake,' she said.

In the conference room that was temporarily the Columbo room they sat down at the table. Captain Sczciegel and Martha joined them, and they called for Geraldo Anselmo.

Martha had brought the news release they planned to distribute today—

The Los Angeles Police Department today announced a major breakthrough in the investigation into the murder of journalist Betsy Clendenin.

A piece of debris hurled far from the Clendenin home by the force of the explosion that killed Miss Clendenin reposed on a rooftop unnoticed until roofers went up to repair the slight damage to the roof. That hunk of debris turned out to be most of the hard-disk drive from Miss Clendenin's computer. Although the drive itself was torn apart and the disks were warped and damaged, a police technician has managed to restore the disks sufficiently well to be able to read most of the data on the disk.

The Department declines to

specify what that data comprises, except to say that it is notes and text relating to a book Miss Clendenin was planning to publish in the near future.

A department spokesman emphasized that the information on the disks was the late Miss Clendenin's work product and as such is the property of her estate. On demand of the executor of her estate, the disks were turned over to him yesterday, on his assurance that they will be returned if needed as evidence in a prosecution.

Columbo read the release. 'There y' go,' he said. 'That oughta smoke somebody out of the woodwork.'

12:22 P.M.

Fritz Kloss heard the report on the noon news—

'We go now to Dick Turner reporting from Parker Center. Dick—'

'Thank you, Chuck. The Police Department this morning announced what may turn out to be a major breakthrough in the mystery surrounding the death by dynamite of famed investigative reporter Betsy Clendenin. A chunk of debris from her blown-apart house rested almost unnoticed on a neighbor's

251

rooftop for more than two weeks before it was plucked from there and turned over to police. That chunk of debris is a hard-disk drive from Clendenin's computer. Almost miraculously, a technician named Geraldo Anselmo has managed to retrieve the data from the damaged disk drive. It reveals what Betsy Clendenin was about to tell in her projected book on the late FBI mogul J. Edgar Hoover. It may, therefore, tell who had motive to murder Betsy Clendenin. The disks have been turned over to her estate and her publisher. The book someone sought to suppress by murder may well be in the bookstores in a few weeks. This is Dick Turner at Police Headquarters. Back to you, Chuck.'

9:00 P.M.

'The next thing I know, you'll be watching my show,' said Meredith. 'Fritz, really . . . You never watched this kind of thing before—not since I've known you.'

'This woman's going to talk about some more slander of the Director. I want to know what filthy lies are going to come out now.'

Meredith sighed. 'Did it ever occur to you that maybe J. Edgar Hoover was not a saint, that maybe he was guilty of some of the things they talk about?'

Fritz's face darkened. 'The Director was one of the finest men this country has ever

252

produced,' he said in a tone that was flat, absolute. 'I don't want to hear any slander of his name.'

'Well, you're going to hear some if you watch this show.'

The commercials ended, and the ebullient host of 'Listening with Don' strode into the set and took his seat behind a desk.

Don Drake, whose real name was Dracovic Kaposvár, was a short, square blond man in a dark-blue double-breasted suit, with a white handkerchief folded in peaks in his breast pocket and a pink carnation in his lapel. He pulled a pair of half-glasses from his inside pocket and donned them for a moment while he squinted over some papers that lay before him, as if he had to remind himself as to whom he was interviewing tonight. He tucked the spectacles back inside his jacket and looked at the camera. 'An excitement is brewing in Los Angeles,' he said. 'This morning LAPD released the information that certain computer disks supposedly destroyed in the explosion that killed the late sensationalist reporter Betsy Clendenin were not in fact destroyed but were blown onto a rooftop several houses away, where they were found and turned over to the homicide detective investigating the murder. A department technician was able to reconstruct the disk drive and recover the data the disks contained. Tonight our guest is a lady who is reading through that data and can tell us something of what it contains. To say the information is scandalous is an understatement.

'Ladies and gentlemen, allow me to introduce a well-known investigative journalist in her own right, Miss Adrienne Boswell!'

Never at a loss for her own personal dramatic flair, Adrienne walked into the set wearing a mini-dress of emerald green, with her red hair lying on her shoulders. When she sat down and crossed her legs her skirt crept back five inches above her knees: a sleek display.

'Another whore,' Fritz muttered sullenly as he stared at the screen.

'Well, Miss Boswell. . . . May I call you Adrienne? What can you tell us? What's on those disks?'

'To begin with, Don, I want to say that the disks were recovered for the LAPD Homicide Squad by Lieutenant Columbo, who is the detective in charge of the investigation. You know, of course, that he was shot and wounded Saturday. But that has to do with another case.'

'Another sensational case!' Drake bubbled. 'We'll have to invite Lieutenant Columbo to be on the show sometime.'

Adrienne smiled. 'You can try. I'm not sure he'd come. He's a modest man, doesn't like much publicity.'

'Anyway, speaking of the disks. What's on

them?'

'Well, you understand they are difficult to read. They are badly damaged. The technician installed them in a new disk drive, but they are in such bad shape that the drive is balky. We've just made a beginning, really, but we can see enough to know that Betsy Clendenin had done an amazing job of investigative reporting.'

'The subject *is* J. Edgar Hoover, isn't it?'

'Oh, yes. And what Betsy found out about him and documented will put a final period on the Hoover myth.'

'Can you be more specific?'

'Well, to start with, Hoover was an egregious racist. Two retired agents quote him almost identically on the subject of Martin Luther King. Allowing a word or two of difference, no more, what he said was, "Martin Luther Coon's no queer. He's just another nigger with an obsession for white women."'

'*He said that?* He said it that way?'

'And more along that line. But there is worse. From time to time over a period of years, J. Edgar Hoover lifted confidential information from FBI files and turned them over to people not authorized to have it, who used it for illegal purposes, specifically to blackmail witnesses and prevent their testifying.'

'Can you name anyone who got this information?'

'I can name two: Roy Cohn and Meyer

Lansky. We'll find other names, I imagine, as we read through the files.'

Drake cocked his head to one side: a characteristic gesture he liked to use. 'Hoover, Cohn, and Lansky are all dead, Adrienne. They can't deny these things. Will there be the names of any *living* people?'

'Definitely,' she said. 'Several men will be named, and maybe someone will sue for libel. We'd welcome that. That would give us the opportunity to question a few people under oath, who ought to be questioned.'

'Is there a possibility that *prosecutions* could come out of this, after all these years?'

'You'll have to ask the Justice Department,' she said. 'I don't know.'

'Do I understand that *you* are in physical possession of these disks?'

'Yes. Technically, they belong to Linda Semon, to whom Betsy Clendenin left them in her will. Linda was Betsy's assistant and her friend. Linda and I have made an agreement. She will do research for me as she did for Betsy, and I will write the story. We will share the credit and the money.'

'A book, after all?'

'No. The explosion didn't destroy these disks, but it destroyed a great deal of other material, which can't be reconstructed. There's enough left for a couple of articles. Walter Mahaffey, who has the book rights, has released his rights to *Glitz*, which is where we'll publish the articles.'

'You've had a busy day, haven't you?'

'Actually, Linda and I had already agreed to do what we could with some notes and her recollections. Probably we'd have gotten one thin article out of that. But of course we've known about the disks since Friday. They were turned over to Linda yesterday.'

'Well, where are the disks? I mean physically.'

'I have them at home. They were installed in a computer we bought for the purpose. One of the priorities, of course, is to copy the data. We'll probably put it on backup tape and put the tape in a vault. The backup machine is being delivered tomorrow.'

Drake grinned. 'Murder will out,' he said.

37

9:32 P.M.

Adrienne waited in Drake's dressing room and office, until he talked about tomorrow night's guest and came off the set. When he came in, she threw her arms around him and kissed him hard on the mouth.

'Dracovic, you're a goddamned gem!' she laughed.

'Did I read my lines good, Miz Boswel?' he drawled.

'Hey! You memorized your script perfectly

and didn't miss a point.'

'Well . . .' He sighed and sat down heavily. 'I hope it works, Adrienne. The guy who blew up Betsy could blow up you.'

10:50 P.M.

Adrienne had invited Dan not to be in her apartment tonight. He understood why but not without both apprehension and resentment.

Martha Zimmer had picked her up in an unmarked car and drove her home. Three other unmarked cars sat on the street, and they radioed assurance that the area was secure. Martha let Adrienne out and drove two blocks away to park her car and walk back.

Inside the apartment, Columbo waited, with Cathy Gray. Cathy was out of uniform but had a Beretta in her shoulder bag. Technicians were at work in the rooms.

'We're gonna feel like a lot of idiots if this doesn't work,' said Columbo. 'I never did put much confidence in settin' traps, and here we've gone to all kinds of trouble to set the most elaborate—What if he doesn't fall for it?'

'We'll all deny we had anything to do with it,' said Adrienne.

'Hey! I'm afraid I've put you in a *hell* of a situation.'

'I've been there before,' she said. 'Hey, I'm gonna have a Scotch. How many?'

'We're all on duty,' said Columbo. 'But

258

maybe just *little* ones.'

Adrienne, Columbo, and Cathy had short drinks of Glenlivet on the rocks—in which Martha joined when she came in.

'We're likely to have a long wait,' Columbo said. 'Maybe all night and nothin'. I mean, maybe I've got it figured all wrong.'

'What is it makes you so sure it's the man you think it is?' Cathy asked.

'Well . . . he told me he never heard the name Harry Lehman. But he put Harry Lehman in Leavenworth for twenty-two years. I don't think he'd forget a thing like that. Then he told me he hadn't been in Las Vegas in many years. But Harry Lehman's son told me the man had been in Vegas just a few weeks ago. Then—Well, maybe the most important thing is that the bomb was set off by a radio signal from a garage-door opener. Those things come with many frequencies. The frequency that set off the bomb also opens the man's garage door. Opens one of his *two* garage doors. Evidence. But I'd like to have a whole lot more, and we gotta depend on the man to present us with it.'

WEDNESDAY, JANUARY 20—2:47 A.M.

The radio came to life and stirred the drowsy crowd in the darkened apartment. 'Unit 468, this is 754. We have an unidentified on the street. Parked his car, walking toward you.'

259

Martha responded. 'Male?'

'Affirmative. Male. Walking briskly, like he knows where he's going.'

'When he makes the door of this building, go to radio silence. We can't have him hearing you.'

'Roger. Understood. And that's now. He's climbing the steps. We'll stand by if you need backup.'

Inside the building, then inside the apartment, police personnel listened as the 'unidentified' defeated the locks. Within a minute and a half he entered the Boswell apartment and stood in the darkness, orienting himself.

Upstairs, Columbo and Adrienne stared at a bank of monitor screens. The apartment seemed dark, but it was bathed in infrared light, and the camcorders mounted at strategic locations were sensitive to infrared light.

Adrienne seized Columbo's right arm. 'Him?' she whispered in his ear.

'I think so. Hard to tell.'

Fritz Kloss appeared as a shadowy green figure on the screens. It would have been difficult to identify him, but what he was doing was abundantly clear.

He explored the first floor of the apartment. Then he drew a gun from his raincoat pocket and mounted the stairs to the second floor.

When he reached the top of the stairs, blinding-bright floodlights illuminated him. He tried to cover his eyes with his left arm.

'Drop the pistol on the floor, Mr. Kloss,' said Martha. 'You are under arrest. You have a right to remain silent—'

EPILOGUE

Fritz Kloss was sentenced to life in prison for the murder of Betsy Clendenin. In view of the fact that he was unlikely to survive his minimum twenty-five years, he was not prosecuted for the murder of Harry Lehman.

Thomas Durant was sentenced to life in prison for the murder of Jason Gimble. No concession was made as to where he might have to serve the time, and he wound up in the prison he most feared: San Quentin. Shortly thereafter, he was severely beaten and was moved into an isolation wing.

Bruce Emerson was sentenced to five years for his role as an accessory to the murders of Edward and Penelope Kent charges to which he pleaded guilty.

Jonathan was sentenced to five years but was allowed to remain outside prison on probation, in view of his delicate health and the fact that he was likely to be abused by other prisoners. It was a condition of his probation that he not touch young girls. Nearly broke, he sold Xanadu and moved into a modest flat in Malibu. On the beach he violated the chief condition of his probation and so faced incarceration. One morning his body washed up on the beach. No one ever knew if he drowned himself or drowned by accident.

In March Columbo and Adrienne appeared as witnesses before a hearing that would make a recommendation to the governor as to whether or not Ai-ling Cooper should be given a commutation of sentence. They met in the hallway outside the hearing room, just before the hearing began. Although she was restrained in handcuffs and a belly chain, Ai-ling strode away from her guards and tearfully greeted her two witnesses. She clasped Columbo's hands and whispered, 'I love you, Lieutenant Columbo!'

Three weeks later her sentence was commuted to time served.

The first of two articles by Adrienne Boswell and Linda Semon appeared in the April issue of *Glitz*. It named Fritz Kloss as the man who had delivered confidential material from FBI files to Roy Cohn and named the retired agent who had told Betsy Clendenin the story. By then Fritz could have cared less.

A media party was held in the *Glitz* offices, followed by a private party in the conference room, where a magnificent spread of food and wine was laid out.

Before they sat down, Ai-ling tapped on a glass and asked for the attention of the room.

'My friends, my many friends,' she said. 'I want to recognize a very special friend in a very special way. Will my friend Lieutenant Columbo please come forward?'

Shyly, Columbo came forward. Adrienne, who knew what was about to happen, came just behind him. Ai-ling gestured, and the tall, dark woman from Pittocco's came from the next room, carrying a jacket identical to the one Columbo had bought with his gift certificate and had lost to the bloodstain from his wound. Adrienne tugged his old jacket off him, and Ai-ling helped him into his new jacket. Then she kissed him.

We hope you have enjoyed this Large Print book. Other Chivers Press or G.K. Hall & Co. Large Print books are available at your library or directly from the publishers.

For more information about current and forthcoming titles, please call or write, without obligation, to:

Chivers Press Limited
Windsor Bridge Road
Bath BA2 3AX
England
Tel. (01225) 335336

OR

G.K. Hall & Co.
P.O. Box 159
Thorndike, Maine 04986
USA
Tel. (800) 223-2336

All our Large Print titles are designed for easy reading, and all our books are made to last.

DATE DUE